CAN'T SHOOT STRAIGHT GANG RETURNS

A HANDSOME ROB GIG

BLAZE WARD

KNOTTED ROAD PRESS

Can't Shoot Straight Gang Returns
A Handsome Rob Gig
Blaze Ward
Copyright © 2018 Blaze Ward
All rights reserved
Published by Knotted Road Press
www.KnottedRoadPress.com

ISBN: 978-1-64470-007-5

Cover art:
ID 75378829 © Angela Harburn | Shutterstock.com

Cover and interior design copyright © 2018 Knotted Road Press

Never miss a release!
If you'd like to be notified of new releases, sign up for my newsletter.

I only send out newsletters once a quarter, will never spam you, or use your email for nefarious purposes. You can also unsubscribe at any time.

http://www.blazeward.com/newsletter/

ALSO BY BLAZE WARD

The Jessica Keller Chronicles

Auberon

Queen of the Pirates

Last of the Immortals

Goddess of War

Flight of the Blackbird

The Red Admiral

St. Legier

Additional Alexandria Station Stories

The Story Road

Siren

The Science Officer Series

The Science Officer

The Mind Field

The Gilded Cage

The Pleasure Dome

The Doomsday Vault

The Last Flagship

The Hammerfield Gambit

The Hammerfield Payoff

Doyle Iwakuma Stories

1

——————

HE SHOULD HAVE KNOWN IT WAS TROUBLE WHEN someone knocked at the door way too early this morning. The sun was barely up. Only cops and reporters got out of bed at dawn.

Handsome Rob opened the door to his apartment by bracing his foot and his shoulder where nobody could knock him back easily. He had a pulse pistol in his hand, down by his side where it wasn't obvious.

Because whoever was out there was still banging loudly, the safety was off.

This was supposed to be his day off. Technically, his whole month off, have just completed another amazing, do-or-die mission for *The Service, Lincolnshire*'s Guardia Civil Interior. Roberto Segura, Field Agent Extraordinaire.

And grumpy dude, mildly hung over as someone didn't have the decency to call on the comm he had silenced last night while drinking so he could sleep in.

Bastards.

He checked the screen showing the hallway. Cursed. Looked again. Cursed again.

The man outside wore a naval uniform. Never a good sign. At least he wasn't Shore Patrol, but an officer.

Robb undid the series of deadbolts, chains, and doorstops so that he could open the door. The knocking ceased when the first lock clunked. Five later, Robb opened the door enough to scowl at the man in the hallway.

"Senior Segura?" the officer asked hopefully.

Unlike Rob, the man was pressed, ironed, and starched to trim perfection. Rob had shaved sometime in the last three days, if he was counting correctly.

Naval Commander, too. In full dress uniform at that. Jacket with ribbons and stuff across the front. Senior enough fellow. Way too important to be a flunky or messenger, unless there was an admiral involved.

"Yeah, that's me," Rob finally answered.

That's what his identity papers said these days, anyway.

Roberto Segora. Six-Foot-One. One-Ninety-Five. Brown eyes. Black Hair. Hispanic genotype.

At least the last five were accurate enough for government work. Which is what he did.

Government work.

"I have a message and papers for you, sir," the commander smiled brightly. "May I come in?"

Rob sighed. A year ago he had been a Courier for the Service. A messenger boy like this commander on his doorstep imitating a damned rooster.

Now he was a Field Agent. Decorated, even, although Jorge and friends had done most of the work. Still, it got him noticed as a man who got things done.

And apparently summoned shits like this guy to come over before lunch.

Rob stepped back quickly enough that the commander couldn't have reacted if he was going to charge. He did keep the pistol handy. And the safety off.

The commander followed him into the room at a polite march, closing the door before Rob could and coming to attention.

Rob felt tired just watching the guy. He looked like the type that had already run ten kilometers this morning, had breakfast, done a pile of paperwork, and then taken a delivery assignment to wake up a secret agent who had been asleep for about three hours at this point.

The man noticed the pulse pistol, but didn't comment, which was good. Carefully, the commander reached into a pocket and pulled out a small packet that he held out carefully.

Rob took it like it might be infected or something.

"Sit," Rob half-ordered, dropping into a chair and gesturing the man to the couch that probably still smelled like the perfume of that gorgeous redhead who had followed him home a few nights ago and had her way with him.

Oh, the sacrifices we make in the *Service*.

Rob cracked open the packet and pulled out the first page.

Seriously?

"Are you fucking kidding me?" Rob asked the man. "They've activated my reserve status and commissioned me as an officer in the *Lincolnshire* Navy? You people do realize who I work for, right?"

At least the commander had to courtesy to look pained at the accusation.

"It is my understanding, sir, that your previous…uhm… experience has been under a civilian rubric," he said carefully. "This operation is apparently falling under the Ministry of Naval Operations and you are being seconded by the Service to them for the time being. You will accrue retirement points and pay, sir, as the commission is being backdated to your original separation date."

Rob fixed the man with an ugly scowl. He liked being an agent of the Service.

Lincolnshire had a puddle-jumper navy, mostly composed of second-hand vessels purchased used from the *Republic of Aquitaine* Navy. Nothing larger than a frigate, since they didn't have the local facilities to build or maintain them, but the galaxy had changed over the last few years.

But apparently stealing an experimental warship from *Salonnia* had brought him to the attention of the right people. And capturing one of *Salonnia*'s senior captains, who had chosen to defect when the alternative was that Jorge would have just shot him out of hand.

Rob wondered if the old commodore had purchased a nicer retirement here by telling more secrets after they dropped the man off.

Rather than answer the commander, Rob looked at the rest of the packet. It had a set of orders with his name at the top.

Investigate a supposedly-new, supposedly-secret naval base one of *Salonnia*'s Crime Syndicates had set up near the juncture of *Lincolnshire*'s space with *Salonnia* and *Corynthe*, the pirate kingdom currently under the sovereignty of an *Aquitaine* admiral named Jessica Keller.

Surveil the facility's capabilities for disrupting trade in the event of active hostilities between nations.

Eliminate said base by whatever means were necessary, while maintaining plausible deniability for *Lincolnshire*.

At least they weren't dreaming too small on this one. One man against an entire naval base, probably with half a dozen little warships set to blow his silly ass up when they caught him.

"Do you have oral orders to supplement these?" Rob asked wearily, standing.

A civilian agent would have been within their rights to

refuse a suicide mission, which was why the first thing those bastards had done was to put him into uniform. Probably figured that would make him a good little Office of Naval Intelligence operative if he wasn't careful.

Of course, if those people hadn't failed in the first place, nobody would have been banging on Rob's door at such an ungodly hour.

"I do not, sir," the man said, also rising. "Instead, I was instructed to give you an hour to get presentable and then drive you to headquarters."

"Do they have an idea of how I'm supposed to do this?" Rob asked, waving the documents. He finally put the safety on, so that he didn't shoot anyone this morning.

"No, sir," the commander grimaced. "I believe the admiral said we were in the Hail Mary stage of things. If this didn't work, we might have to beg *Aquitaine* for another Jessica Keller, or something."

Rob matched the man's grimace. A decade ago, she had blown up a pirate base on the surface of a planet not all that far from there by hitting it with an asteroid. En route to conquering all of *Corynthe* with a couple of tiny warships and a lot of audacity.

Audacity.

Rob smiled so suddenly that the commander took a defensive step back unconsciously.

"Sir?" he asked.

"*Audacity*," Rob grinned. "That's what this is going to take."

"And?" the commander asked carefully.

"I might know a guy."

2

———

For a day that had started out too early, and then spent too much time inside a dreary office building, the evening wasn't looking too bad. Rob had placed a call when he managed to escape the various captains and admirals looking to him to save the day, and then got a repulsor-taxi that hadpicked him up at the front gate of the naval base and hauled him into town.

Puerto Peñasco hadn't changed in the last year. Or maybe the last fifty. The city looked like all cities outside of major naval bases, in every star nation he had ever visited. Blue collar for the most part. Worn down and a little seedy. Just this side of a crime-ridden slum, if you turned the wrong way at the wrong intersection.

The place where the taxi dropped Rob took him back nearly a year, to where it had all started. His first mission as a Field Agent. At the top of a staircase to a below-street dive, two blocks from *El Ayuntamiento*. In the wrong direction.

The inside of the bar was just as old and decrepit as it had been then, somehow hanging on at the very edge of not quite run down enough to be demolished for something better. A

7

battered wooden bar on one side, where thirty people could sit, instead of the dozen or so there now.

Booths on the left, slightly elevated on a walkway to give a view over the tables on the floor, at the stage where live music frequently played. It was Tuesday, so Rob hoped fervently that it wasn't open mic night. Or Ladies Night.

Or anything that involved dealing anymore with random, needy strangers.

His contact was seated in that same, central booth as before, with conspicuously-empty ones on either side.

Jorge Royo. Famous video star who had once been a serious thespian, before he moved into campy, over-the-top action comedies, frequently ones that he wrote, produced, and directed, just so he could work with his friends. And keep most of the money himself.

Even the Service wasn't entirely sure what Jorge was worth these days.

Late fifties, at first glance, but Rob knew now that the man was at least a decade older. Hair starting to gray on the sides, after decades of dye to keep it dead black as a leading man. A little work around the face to keep things tight. The galaxy's most famous sun tan revealed by a peach silk shirt half unbuttoned.

In his hand, Jorge held a martini glass. It was almost his signature move these days.

Jorge smiled as Rob got close. The noise inside was quiet enough that they could talk.

"Vishnu, kid, you look like hell," Jorge greeted him, waving an arm to get the attention of a buxom, bottle-blond, bar maid with a fantastic ass. *Tallia.*

Rob remembered her from a year ago as well, surprised that she still worked in a dump like this. The money must be better than one expected from the clientele.

Rob sat. Well, more collapsed into the booth beside Jorge

and let the weight of the day flow off to infect some of the other people in the room.

Tallia came close, her shirt buttoned just enough to make her prominent chest utterly distracting as she smiled at him.

"Whiskey, neat?" she asked. "Top shelf?"

Rob tried not to goggle too badly. She hadn't seen him in a year and remembered what he drank? In a bar he had been in exactly twice before this?

"And another for me," Jorge swirled his martini glass a touch and them emptied it.

Rob would have thought that Jorge was a drunk, but he had seen the man consume enough alcohol to kill a moose without achieving hardly more than a good buzz. And he was a happy drunk, at that.

Maybe the man was immune to alcohol, like some doctor had added an extra filter to his stomach that just routed most of it into his bladder instead of his bloodstream.

"So talk to me, kid," Jorge instructed him. "Your call sounded messy. Usually the Service handles these things, but you were coming here directly from ONI? What gives?"

Habit and training made Rob scan the immediate area for eavesdroppers before he spoke. This was technically a public place, but the locals knew to stay away from Jorge without invitation.

"Some Salonnian Syndicate has a new base out where they shouldn't be," Rob replied in a quiet voice, pitched so that only Jorge would hear. "The usual things have failed, so the fleet panicked and asked the Service for *Extraordinary Measures.*"

"How bad?" Jorge leaned a little closer.

"I am now on active duty with the *Lincolnshire* Navy, as a Lt. Commander." Rob mostly kept the snarl out of his voice. "With orders to do something about it. And I've just spent the entire, damned day dealing with a bunch of admirals, captains, and headless chickens, so I needed a drink. Thought I'd see if you had any ideas, since we were both in town at the same time."

"How wide is your writ for action?" Jorge's face turned serious.

Dangerously serious. The man had been a famous vid star for a decade, and then a successful B- and C-level actor for another three, but he was also one of the Service's secret weapons, an agent whose antics were so gonzo that nobody realized the man was a spy.

Like the time a year ago when Rob helped Jorge and his friends steal a warship right out of a *Salonnian* naval base, in the middle of a rock concert. Under the guise of scouting to make a pirate movie.

"Probably as wide as I want to push it," Rob replied after a moment. "If I want to get stupid."

Tallia returned with drinks, interrupting the conversation before she retired. Unlike the first time Rob had been in here, there was no banter or innuendo between her and Jorge tonight, so maybe she was much smarter than she looked and could read the audience's need for quiet.

"Did you ever end up making that movie?" Rob continued, holding the glass and just smelling the whiskey. "*Can't Shoot Straight Gang?*"

"No," Jorge smiled. "Got sidetracked at first, and then the damned Service wouldn't come down on their price for rights to film it. Apparently, they realized that it might make money. Still want to work on it if we do?"

"Absolutely," Rob felt some of the weight fall of his shoulders for the first time in what felt like hours. "If they'll let me. The Service, that is. Or the Navy."

"Thinking about getting the band back together?" Jorge's smile apparently was infectious.

"Maybe," Rob took a sip of the amazingly excellent

whiskey and let the liquid, caramelized smoke coat his insides with a layer of warm. It reminded him that he hadn't eaten anything but a breakfast burrito today, as well. "Need food. But need some help trying to come up with something. I cannot imagine a con that gets me or us onto a secret naval base. At least, not a second time. They're probably still a little pissed about the first."

"Oh, they are," Jorge laughed. "Not the government, exactly, but the Syndicate that funded that ship. They were out everything, and *Lincolnshire*'s been trying to reverse engineer it instead. That vessel is now one of the heaviest ships in *Lincolnshire*'s whole fleet, at least until the new designs come on line."

"New designs?" Rob felt his mind perk back up. He wasn't a naval spy, but data became information after you churned it around long enough.

"War Catamarans," Jorge leaned back and sipped his martini. "Take two old frigates and build a bridging element across the center, like a capital H. Put some heavy weapons on that mount so you don't have to rebuild the bows of the older vessels, and you have something up in the medium to heavy cruiser range. At least the old range. Not sure how they rank against *Aquitaine*'s new Expeditionary Cruisers."

Rob thought about it for a moment, but then shook his head.

"No, don't tell me how you know these things," Rob said. "Better off not knowing."

Jorge smiled like a sphinx.

"So you want me to make some calls and see who's in town?" Jorge asked.

"Dinner's on the Ministry's creditstik," Rob smiled cruelly. "At the fanciest place you can swindle a reservation."

"Kid, you shouldn't challenge me like that, you know,"

Jorge laughed. "I might be a third-rate actor, but I'm still a first-rate conman."

"That's why I called, Jorge."

"And your thoughts on a con job?" Jorge grinned. "How it will never work?"

"Yeah?"

"That's because you're conning the wrong people."

3

Because he was pissed at the whole situation and most of the galaxy, Handsome Rob had decided to live up to the nickname Jorge had given him, and treated himself to a day at a luxury spa after getting himself measured for a brand new tuxedo.

Not his creditstik. Not his budget.

He emerged looking like a million dinars, and dressed like it as well. Even his pulse pistol was nearly invisible in the jacket's perfect cut.

A ground vehicle was waiting when he walked out the front door of the spa, where he had been expecting his repulsor-taxi in the front quad. He hadn't ordered a limousine tonight, but the back door opened and Aphrodite emerged from the sea as he watched.

Her real name was Roxanne, but nobody outside a small group ever called her that or even Roxy. She had spent the better part of two decades as the principle stuntwoman for *Mrs. Jones*, one of the most famous actresses in the galaxy, before that worthy woman had *moved on* to more cerebral and so-called serious roles. The kind that didn't involve close-combat martial arts, combat driving, or small arms expertise.

These days, with the right makeup, a big hat, and sunglasses, she was Mrs. Jones, and had played that part for Jorge on several operations, where misdirection was the key. Everyone wanted to fall all over themselves to be near the most beautiful woman in the galaxy.

Roxy was amazing looking, all by herself, but she was all muscle and brains under those curves, and on their last mission together, had been impersonating a nymphomaniac. And she'd needed Rob's help to get into character.

He couldn't help but smile as he saw her. The late afternoon sun made it a pleasant, tropical day in the mid-eighties. Roxy was wearing white today. A dress slit nearly to her hip bone on one side, mostly backless, and with just enough front to contain her chest for polite company. As always, she was without tan lines on all the visible parts, which was most of them.

Just for the hell of it, Rob walked right up and kissed the woman. Probably the worst she would do right now was punch him, but she returned the kiss fervently before breaking it and grinning.

"Now everyone will be jealous," she laughed quietly, looking over his shoulder, where Rob was sure he had an awe-struck audience on the other side of the glass windows.

Rob laughed and handed her back into the back of the vehicle before climbing in himself and pulling the door shut.

Jorge was already there, on the other side of Roxy. He could make a tuxedo and an undone tie look perfectly appropriate in any situation, and did.

Across the way, facing rear, sat Longbow, aka Levi Framingham the musician, dressed well but not as well and smiling. At least the unfortunate, blond flattop had grown out over the last year into something vaguely businesslike.

Next to the musician was *Raef*. Rafaela Dominguez, captain of the Private Service Yacht *Valencia del Oro*. She was almost Rob's height, but built more like a scarecrow than an athlete. Unlike Roxy's hard curves and dangerous muscles, Raef was skinny and kinda homely, but a first rate navigator. She shared Rob and Jorge's Hispanic heritage in the black hair just starting to gray and brown eyes broad and laughing much of the time.

Tonight, she had stepped away from being a captain, wearing a simple black sheath in silk that made her legs look three miles long. With her shoulder-length hair loose and brushed back, she looked like a tree that a squirrel might enjoy climbing. Longbow had that look in his eyes.

The interior partition was down, and Rob spotted Nigel's cowboy hat up front on the driver as the ground vehicle pulled away from the curb with a smooth burst of acceleration.

"Did I buy this or is it stolen?" Rob asked Jorge in a serious innocence. Never admit to being an accomplice, even unknowing and after the fact.

"Neither," the man grinned. "People owe me favors. Or want to get on my list."

"Good enough," Rob nodded to everyone. "Surprised that the whole gang was available on two days' notice."

Roxy had curled herself up against his side in a distracting way. Gods, that woman smelled even more amazing than he remembered.

"A little pixie might have whispered in my ear a few weeks ago," Jorge grinned, lifting his martini glass from what looked like a custom stem holder. "Suggested the powers that be might be starting to panic, as it were. I put the word out, just in case."

"I see," Rob grinned back. "Thank you. We'll talk more at dinner, after I have hopefully sufficiently bribed all of you, because this one's even bigger and crazier than stealing *Silverfish*."

Roxy looked up at him with the most innocent eyes ever.

"You'll have to ask me extra special nice to do something like that for you, Handsome," she purred as the other folks in back laughed.

Seriously, no man was safe around this woman. And probably most women, if she set her mind to it.

Longbow handed him a highball of whiskey that matched the one the guitarist was holding.

"Let's get crazy, kid," Longbow toasted him and they both drank.

Roxy grabbed Rob's glass and took a sip as well, while Jorge enjoyed what appeared to be a bottomless, or at least never-ending martini and Raef drank wine

Quickly enough, Nigel pulled them up at the base of a tower. They were still in Puerto Peñasco, barely, right along that line where the naval base gave way to the city, except that they were outside the gate closer to officers' quarters, and well down from where the enlisted partied.

Rob handed Roxy and Raef up as every person in sight stopped to stare, doubly so as Jorge emerged from the other side and Longbow joined them. Nigel would park the beast and be along shortly, not trusting a valet with these wheels.

The elevator seemed intent on reaching orbit, but they were in truth only going up sixty stories. Still, Roxy had attached herself to his side with a lascivious grin that just made up for the rest of the week.

Now they just had to do the impossible. And survive to tell.

Handsome Rob did not ask how Jorge had managed reservations here tonight. From his limited understanding of things, the list went out approximately six months in advance.

And yet they were seated in a private room located just behind the bar and next to the kitchen, with their own dedicated waiter and bartender poised for service. Rob let his decadence stretch just a little bit when they ordered. He didn't really *need* a one kilo ribeye steak. Nor the grilled shrimp on the side. He did need something to drink, and the cost per bottle on this whiskey was high enough to make him smile.

Nigel and Longbow both went all in, as well.

Smiling at his friends, dinner tonight would possibly run into roughly what he got paid on a monthly basis, in a nice gig as a Field Agent. Not quite the top of the tiers for service salary, but not down with the little people.

Of course, his budget for a mission this insane was probably a frighteningly high number, if he decided to push. That might yet come, but first he wanted to treat his friends well.

Rob ordered the Tiramisu and the Crème Brulee with fruit, just so Roxy could have delicate nibbles off both, acting like a wee, little kitten so innocent you blushed on her behalf.

It was all a ploy. Rob knew she could bench press his weight.

Rob toasted Jorge and the others with a glass of whiskey almost as good as what Tallia brought.

"The other day, you mentioned conning the wrong people, Jorge," Rob paused to belch, grin, and then sip some more. "Who are the right people?"

"So the bosses want something like this done with plausible deniability, as always, right?" Jorge asked. "Complete misdirection and all that. That's why they hire us to handle the big things. You can hide an amazing amount of deceit by pretending to be larger than life movie stars."

"With you so far, but no sure where that's taking us on

this one," Rob gestured with his whiskey glass to the others, all eyes around the table bright and focused.

"I had considered one of the other Syndicates as my patsies," Jorge finished a martini, just as the waiter arrived with a replacement and departed wordlessly. "That way, everybody over there is mad at each other. As you know, they aren't really a government so much as a bunch of crime bosses that own politicians, so that's always a seam we can exploit. But we should dream bigger. Crazier."

"Oh, shit, you're really going to do it this time, aren't you?" Longbow asked. "After threatening it for more than a decade?"

"Worse," Jorge practically preened. "We all owe Rob one from last time, so we're going to play straight men on this one, and he's pulling the con."

Roxy stopped being the dead-sexy movie star and turned back into a stuntwoman as she sized Rob up with new eyes.

"You think they'll go for it?" she asked, but it was obvious she was talking to Jorge.

Rob felt lost. Way lost.

"The kid's a natural," Jorge said. "You all know that. And we can use that to our advantage. Where will they naturally look?"

"Uhm," Rob managed to interrupt the flow before he drowned in it. "What exactly are we talking about here?"

"You tell him, Roxy," Jorge prodded the woman.

She turned and fixed Jorge with a catlike scowl, like maybe a mouse was getting presumptuous. Jorge appeared as immune as ever.

"So our dear leader has had this fantastic scam that he has always wanted to pull," she explained. "However, by the time we got all the moving parts established, the world had changed, and it was no longer appropriate, except in a worst case scenario. Apparently, he's either suffering from mental decline, or wants to go out with a bang, because there's almost no way this works in the current political climate."

"Yup," Rob nodded absently and sipped. "Still lost."

"He wants to go con the pirates of *Corynthe* into doing it," she grinned a little lopsided at him, like it was an apology.

Rob studied her face. Jorge's. Longbow. Nigel.

It was perfectly insane. So completely off the charts that the Service would probably teach it as a special class in Field Agent school. Whether that was to repeat it, or never make that mistake again remained to be seen.

But after a moment, all the pieces fell into alignment. Rob didn't think his face had changed, but Jorge smiled.

"Yes," the con artist smiled. "You see it. What do you think?"

"I think we need a better script," Rob grinned at the man. "*Can't Shoot Straight Gang Returns.*"

4

<hr>

Valencia del Oro was a lovely yacht that Handsome Rob approved of. Like last time, Jorge and Mrs. Jones had the two master suites, located at either end of the long-skinny ship, with Jorge a deck above the engines and Mrs. Jones above the bridge with wraparound windows that covered three-quarters of the suite when you opened all the shades. The other three of them, along with Raef, had four of the six cabins on the main deck, a right turn towards the front end.

Rob was even in his old cabin when he boarded, but fortunately for his relative sanity, it was empty when he entered. Not that he would have minded a good romp with Roxy, but it wasn't that kind of mission. Presumably. Still, a white rose left on his pillow, without any note, suggested that perhaps the woman had had the same thoughts.

He did smile as he headed aft to the main lounge, looking to find the others back there. Rob had a suspicion many had been aboard for a few days, just waiting for him. Not that he minded.

The lounge had a kitchen on one side and a booth big enough for a dozen friends on the other. Coffee was ready and waiting for him as he entered

Jorge was already drinking coffee and reading something on a table as Rob watched, but there was a martini glass close, like perhaps the man needed it for fuel on a regular basis. With his career and reputation, Jorge could do whatever he wanted.

Rob grabbed a black coffee today, rather than whiskey, laughing to himself as he sat next to Jorge and remembered the last mission. Jorge had consumed martinis morning, noon, and night. Longbow had been experimenting with all manner of narcotics to find the perfect blend for his cover as a drug-crazed rock star. Nigel had spent time aft in the machine bay, building things that ended up never being used but made him smell like a pyromaniac.

And Roxy had spent the entire flight getting into character. As a nymphomaniac. In his cabin. At least she still smiled at him when she wasn't playing that character.

Longbow wandered in a few quiet minutes later, with Roxy right behind him.

"Raef says three minutes to lift, if we want to strap in," the musician smiled as he grabbed a sippy cup mug and poured coffee, coconut cream, coconut oil, and honey in, sealing it and shaking hard.

"Any warrants out for her arrest?" Jorge looked up at Longbow.

"Not that she's told me about," the man replied innocently.

"Then I don't feel the need to batten down the hatches just to take off," Jorge smiled and went back to his tablet, about the time Rob was considering how hot a liftoff they might have if she needed to outrun the law.

You never knew, especially not with this crew.

Roxy smiled at Rob from across the table when she sat, but she was all business today. *Valencia del Oro* lifted with just the slightest surge in the lights and motion as the ship leaned back and ran like hell for outer space.

Nigel and Raef entered from opposite ends of the ship at almost the same moment after a few minutes of small talk later. Nigel poured two mugs of coffee while Raef sat her remote piloting tablet on the table and slid into the big booth next to Rob.

"You're probably wondering why I've called you all together like this," Jorge smiled at the group as everyone laughed, groaned, or in Roxy's case, punched him on the shoulder.

"I've always loved that line," Jorge said. "So utterly cheesy and trite, especially when you can deliver it deadpan in a comedy movie. Raef, what did you find out about our target?"

Rob felt a bit of whiplash has he turned to the tall woman on his left.

"Last anyone knew, nothing had changed," she said cryptically. "Most recent intel is about six months old, so it might be a complete cluster when we get there, but he's been in charge for five years, give or take, so make of it what you will."

Raef wasn't one for long speeches, so Rob was a little shocked. That might be the most words he had heard her speak in one breath.

"Good enough," Jorge replied. "We've never met as part of a swindle, he and I, at least as far as I know, so no reason he won't fall for it. Though in fact, I might have met him twenty years ago when I did something on *Callumnia*, if it's the same guy. Do we know?

"Nephew of the old Governor," Raef said. "Former captain of a boat named *Dragonfly*."

"Son of a gun, I do know him," Jorge snapped. "At least sort of. If he remembers me. That might give us an in. Rob, you ready?"

"I've read your notes and destroyed them, Jorge," Handsome replied. "Seems straightforward enough. Can we really trust a pirate to keep his word on something like this? Will he even go for it, or just take us all hostage for whatever ransom he figures he can get?"

"Ah, my boy, you're getting sharp, but you've only just begun to scratch the surface of a good, rolling con," Jorge laughed. "The trick is to keep them on the hook for an even bigger payoff later. Most people won't strike immediately, because greed turns their head. That's how pyramid schemes work, if you're smart enough to get out early, before it collapses. After that first taste, you just keep spinning tales. It's like hooking a big fish. You got to tease him into the boat, since he's too large to just drag over. Pull a little, and then let him run, but each time pull a little more than he gets away. He gets tired, and closer."

"And eventually you gaff him alongside and beat the crap out of him with a big club," Roxy smiled and joined the conversation. "Works on fish, too."

Everyone laughed, but there was an element of tenseness under the notes. That was the problem with stakes this high. There was always an element of risk.

It wasn't like you could just order up a strike squadron to storm in overhead, damning the torpedoes and the costs. *Lincolnshire* didn't have a fleet like that. *Aquitaine* did, but needed a reason to help out, and a surprise ambush of a foreign base on foreign soil wouldn't do the trick. Especially since everyone was supposedly at peace.

Theoretically.

"So we're just going to sail up to a pirate base and ask for help?" Rob kept most of the sarcasm out of his voice.

"Oh, it's almost the same con as we pulled to steal *Silverfish,* but we've got a better script this time," Longbow spoke up. "And every space pirate likes to think of himself as a romantic figure, rather than a cutthroat criminal. Plus, Keller did a number on those bastards, back in the day, and the worst of them either got killed, retired, or ran off someplace she couldn't find them. Her fleet came through and scared the living shit out of anybody with second thoughts a couple of years after that, without her. Raef, what's traffic like these days?"

Rob watched the byplay closely. Last time, they had all been into their characters already by this point, relying on him to play the straight man in complete ignorance of their scam. This time, he was part of the team. Growing up at the feet of these masters, as it were, all of them two or three decades older than him.

Wiser. Sneakier. Meaner.

"*Lincolnshire*'s actually a little worse than *Corynthe,* these days," the captain brightened up from her scowl. "More smuggling and penny-ante stuff on any given day. Bribes for passage and fast clearance against bureaucracy. If a *Corynthe* pirate is feeling hungry, though…"

That much, Rob understood. Most of his missions over the last year had been subtle ones. Sneak in and deliver messages or equipment to spies already in place, or get defectors out quietly. To date, he had still never shot anyone, although he trained and qualified with a dozen different weapons every month. From Field Agent, the next step up in responsibility was Assassin.

"And that's my general point," Jorge took up the center of the conversation again. "We go in as wide-eyed kids, playing to their masculinity and awesome pirateness. Every man's ego gets a little puffed up and they maybe stop paying attention to the little things. Throw in a little greed, and maybe dangle some movie star glamor. You saw how that worked before, Rob."

"Audacity," Rob agreed. "So big and crazy that nobody actually believes that it's not the truth, until it bites you on the ass."

"You got it," Roxy grinned. "Mrs. Jones and I don't actually look all that much alike in the face, but they never get past the chest and ass enough to pay attention, just remembering that poster they maybe had on their bedroom wall as a teenager. They want to believe the lie, because it gets them close to this,"

Everyone else laughed as the woman stood halfway up and gestured to her body, like a used repulsorlift salesman with a mark on the hook. But Rob had to agree. He'd seen it in action.

"Okay," Jorge said. "Three weeks hard haul gets us to the our pirates," Jorge said. "We've got the standard equipment package aboard: special effects, both personal weapons and stuff we've hidden in Longbow's gear, and a script. I'll expect you to be in character three days before we land, and hold to those. And try to keep the egos in check this time. Remember, we're poor, broke, and desperate for some cheap labor to help us film this movie. Questions?"

"What if they actually provide a Director of Photography and a full film crew?" Rob perked up and asked. I mean, what *was* the worst that could happen?

"Kid, you figure out how to sneak them into position and I'll make the damned movie, starting with whatever footage we can salvage of however we manage this stunt," Jorge's face got serious. "A lot of the rest of it can be done on a soundstage, or we can borrow a couple of ships from folks I know for interior photography."

Rob grinned at the man. So did the rest. They knew Jorge was serious. He could always get funding to finish the reshoots necessary to turn good stock footage into a movie.

Now, he just had to con a planetful of pirates into signing up as extras and bit players.

5

THE DOOR TO HIS PRIVATE CHAMBER WAS LOCKED AND barred. Fiongall *Finn* Fukui didn't really think that he would have to deal with assassins, but he also kept a prudent level of paranoia around certain things. As Governor of *6940 Draconis*, he had made enough enemies over his lifetime.

So the banging on the door might be trouble, and it might simply be that he had turned off the comm last night because it was supposed to be his day of rest today, and someone needed something that Steafan couldn't deal with himself or push off until tomorrow.

Finn sighed heavily as Aoki rolled over sleepily.

"Your turn," she laughed quietly.

It was an old joke. Both of their kids were grown and gone nearly a decade now, working on their own families and trying to figure out how to get little ones to sleep through the night.

Finn rolled out of bed and, just because, grabbed a bolter pistol from inside his nightstand. He checked that it was loaded. The air in their bedroom was kept a little colder, because Aoki liked it that way, so he slept in loose pants and

29

a shirt that were good enough for whoever wanted to bother him at…ye gods, who the hell needed him at three-fifty-three in the morning?

"Who is it?" Finn walked into the main room and keyed the comm, having moved to one side of the door, in case it was an assassination and bullets were about to impact on the steel-core door.

At least the knocking ceased.

"Steafan," came the reply. "Someone just made orbit and sent an urgent message to, and I quote: *Finn Fukui, Governor General of 6940 Draconis and Grand Poobah of the Outer Reaches*, unquote."

Okay, that was a pretty old joke, so whoever it was thought they had a connection from the days before he was Governor and wanted to remind him. Or at least call it to mind. He had introduced himself to the world that way for a year or so when he took over the Two-Ring Mothership *Dragonfly*.

Who the hell wanted to talk to him that couldn't wait?

"Why do I need to be awake, Steafan?" Finn leaned close enough to the comm so that he could talk normally.

"Jorge Royo and friends would like a private audience," Steafan continued. "And they want to talk about filming a movie here, with all the tax incentives, write-offs, and accounting gimmicks that go with it. They claim that time and secrecy are of the essence."

He opened the door and stared at his right hand assistant, what other places might call his Chief of Staff, but Steafan Sìoltach still went by the title of First Officer, even though neither of them were shipboard pirates anymore. If there was such a thing in the era of *Jessica I, Queen of the Pirates*.

Steafan wasn't as tall as Finn. Hadn't really been a good

knife fighter, back in the day. Oh, he was still reedy and fast as a mongoose. Head kept shaved these days instead of having a bald ring. But his brains and ability to outthink and outmaneuver a foe had been why he had risen as he had, and why he stayed with Finn when they went into administration.

"Jorge Royo? The movie star?" Finn let the sleepiness wash off him now.

He had met the man once. Maybe twenty years ago, back when Finn was a hot-shot captain on a Two-Ring Mothership. Back when Finn's uncle got elected Governor of Callumnia. Back when he did call himself Grand Poobah of the Outer Reaches.

"And friends," Steafan said with a perfectly straight face. "They included a couple of publicity stills. Mrs. Jones is apparently aboard, as well as a guy named Longbow."

Longbow's here?

Finn still had an album he had bought twenty years ago, back when the guy was the biggest thing in music in this entire octant. One of his favorite things to put on and listen to when he did paperwork in the evening and Aoki was in a different room.

Finn reminded himself not to be starstruck. Much. He was also important and famous people these days.

But still…

"You landing them yet?" Finn asked.

"Haven't, pending your opinion," Steafan replied with a grin. "They could be on the ground in three hours for an early breakfast, or I can slot you in for brunch. Or they can wait until tomorrow. Figured that Longbow was worth waking you up, since someone decided to wake me up, thinking this was an emergency."

Yeah, Steafan knew about Longbow. Didn't listen to his music, being more of a Classical Pulse Pop fan when he thought nobody was watching. Still, perks of being Grand Poobah of the Outer Reaches, and all that.

"Make it brunch," Finn decided. "Here in the palace so we can control the gossip until we know what they're up to. Wasn't there some stink a while back about a concern in *Salonnia*?"

"Dunno, but I'm awake so I'll roust your intelligence people and put them to work," Steafan replied. "Anybody I should invite to this one?"

"No, let's be private for now," Finn said. " You, me. Aoki if she wants, but she probably won't. We can always hold a lottery later for tickets to a State Dinner, if they want to turn this into a three-ring-circus. I'm going to go work out for a while, and then be in the office in a few hours."

"See you then with updates."

Finn closed the door as Steafan retreated down the hall. He went back into the bedroom and secured the pistol before sliding back into bed.

"Your hands are cold," Aoki complained as he curled up against her back. "And I heard you tell Steafan you were going to the gym. I'm sleeping in."

Finn laughed and rolled back out of bed. A quick change and then he'd go assuage the gods of exercise before facing the demons of paperwork.

And then he would have lunch with a couple of certified movie stars and a rock star.

As well as see what they hell they wanted with *6940 Draconis*.

6

———————

Seriously, the surface of this planet reminded him of a bad parts of the desert just inland from Puerto Peñasco. And as near as Rob could tell, the rest of the planet was even worse. Arid and dry, with a few, landlocked oceans, subject to temperature extremes that made him wonder why anybody bothered to settle here.

It wasn't as though there weren't a bunch of planets, even out here on the fringes of the galaxy, already habitable, having been terraformed in the days of the ancients. Why would anyone want nights barely above freezing and days that got to one hundred and thirty degrees regularly?

Sure, there was mining. All sorts of odd, exotic metals and materials fairly close to the surface, apparently from a nearby supernova at the right time, billions of years ago. Maybe that sort of thing was worth digging, since you could mostly live underground and climate control things easy enough, with a sea of solar cells above, clustered around a bunch of bunkers that looked like ant nests from any distance. Still, at least forty or fifty million people called this rock and the orbital stations home.

Valencia del Oro was in a pretty good landing slot, compared to where they could have been. And the field was weird, with underground tunnels everywhere like giant rabbits or moles had lived here. You landed in a big pit and a tunnel would extend to more or less meet you.

Wasn't an airlock, because you still had to walk about fifteen feet from door to door in open air, but that was far enough that you didn't roast or freeze, if you didn't dawdle.

But it was a weird planet, nonetheless.

Rob had dressed like a traveling salesman for this one. Flashier suit than a Field Agent on a mission. Shiny and almost useless in a distracting way, to use the term his trainers had instilled in him. Like lawyers, or pimps, if you could separate the two enough to get sunlight between them. Of course, some pimps probably took exception to the comparison.

Jorge and Roxy had gone for understated glamor today. Two past-their-prime superstar actors looking for one last gig. Longbow looked like they had liberated him from the hospital or morgue and grabbed the first shirt and pants they could grab in a darkened closet. At least Nigel looked normal. Raef was staying with the ship until Jorge decided he needed her in person. She was probably the smartest one here, on that count.

Into the tube, they followed the landing instructions that had been transmitted and walked a couple hundred yards along a tunnel that honestly looked like any space station Rob had ever visited. At the far end, a small, automated train awaited them, whooshing them across the underside of the landing field to the capital palace for their reception.

Apparently, the dude in charge really was the same guy, and he did remember being called *Grand Poobah* happily enough to welcome them. Hopefully.

Rob was armed, just in case, but that was business, not

need. Most of the rest of them probably were as well, but that was just careful prudence on a planet of pirates. Or however these folks introduced themselves these days.

The train was automated, so they rode in companionable silence, deep in character. Jorge and Mrs. Jones were movie stars. Longbow was a down-on-his-luck musician doing soundtracks to survive these days. Nigel was the group's gopher and personal assistant.

And Handsome Rob was the con artist selling these poor schmucks on a con of his own. Which was funny when he considered how long some of these folks had been grifting. Still, they would make it work.

They arrived at the main station, a vast, underground vault with low ceilings and many mole tunnels disappearing into the walls with tracks. A well-dressed, bald gentleman awaited when the car stopped, smiling as they emerged, his suit something extremely light-weight and well-cut, however taupe the fabric.

"I bring you our Governor's greetings. I am Steafan Sìoltach, First Officer to the Governor," the man said floridly, somehow managing to look smarmy and malevolent at the same time.

Maybe that was just Rob, hopefully being in character.

"Greetings in return," Rob said, introducing everyone. "My name is Roberto Segura, representing Blue Wave Films and Señior Jorge Royo. Mrs. Jones. Levi Framingham. Nigel Phipps."

"I am pleased to meet all of you," Sìoltach replied. "If you will follow me, we have arranged brunch with the Governor at the palace."

Rob felt that a smile was appropriate for the grifting chiseler he was playing, so he let that sort of thing take up residence on his face as the First Officer led them to a different train. This one got unlocked with a fob extracted from the man's pocket and replaced to open the door. The machine was already programmed, apparently.

Or it only had one destination. You never knew when everything was underground.

Rob figured that Jorge and Roxy had both already calculated the best way to separate the device from the owner, but, knowing Nigel, he had scanned the signal and the frequency and stored it against future use.

The man never talked much, but there was never any doubt when he was on information security systems.

They rode in companionable small talk. The lack of weather. Recent planetfalls. Exciting local news, what there might be of it.

The palace was, disappointingly, just another subway tram stop, with a station done in the same white or black tile as the others, with only *PALACE* on two walls to indicate you had made it to the right place.

Still, they were here. The same fob opened a locked door that led to something of a security airlock.

Sìoltach beeped.

"Oh my," he said theatrically. "I'm afraid that you will not be allowed to carry your personal weapons into the brunch audience. A guard will be awaiting us on the far side with claims tickets."

A touch overdone, if anything. Probably not the first time this man had gone through this speech. After all, *Corynthe* prided itself on being a land of pirates, however semi-reformed and law-abiding they might claim to be these days.

A good governor, the kind who had managed to stay in power for six years, was most likely expecting assassins or troublemakers.

At least they were going to be polite about it.

The inner door opened, revealing a large, impersonal

chamber and a half-dozen men with guns in holsters, none of whom resembled the Governor.

Rob figured he might as well settle things early, so he turned to his right and carefully withdrew the pulse pistol, handing it to a hard-looking woman with a checklist, in trade for a ticket. Jorge followed, then Nigel, then Longbow.

Roxy just smiled serenely, almost beatifically.

Interestingly, she didn't draw out the holdout pistol Rob knew she had on her, but the locals didn't say anything, so they must have missed it in their scans. She could get to it easy enough, just by showing off a flash of thigh and the spot where her garter belt snapped to her white, thigh-high stockings.

Good to know she still had it. Must be one of Nigel's toys. Rob wondered how many other such undetected devices there were in the party.

"Very good, madam and gentlemen," Sìoltach carried on as if nothing had interrupted their conversation. "If you would follow me?"

He led them to a closed, double door. It was old and made of wood, from the weight and look, which meant it had been imported from off-planet, just to separate this room from the rest of the palace. That was a useful tidbit Rob filed he followed the man into a smaller space, almost a drawing room, set with one longish table and already prepared for breakfast.

Now the fun part of the scam could unfurl. Down on their luck movie stars hoping for a little verisimilitude in their next feature. Maybe borrow a small squadron of ships and accidentally talk them into going a little overboard. A pirate romance designed to make the troublesome barbarians of *Corynthe* over into terribly-misunderstood bad boys, the kind that make the good girls swoon and think about running away from the abbey. Bit parts for important financiers and politicians. Tax breaks and matching funds.

All the sorts of things that Rob had spent a lot of time studying over the last year, then boning up on as they flew out into the wilderness.

The Governor rose as they entered. Older man, perhaps early fifties, but still fit and muscular. Longish, curly black hair was graying in stripes that probably acted to carbonate the hormones of most women, as his face had that perfect blend of rugged and handsome that would likely hold in place for another decade or two before fading, much like Rob's father and both grandfathers had managed.

The man appeared taller than Rob, perhaps by an inch. Heavier, too, with obvious muscles from lifting weights, where Rob generally concentrated on fluid mobility in his strength training.

The man was wearing a blazer-style jacket, but instead of a dress shirt and a tie, he seemed to be wearing a simple, black T-shirt underneath. The top was faded from the original black, almost to gray. Washed too many times, would be Rob's guess, but kept as a favored treasure.

The front had a print of a much-younger Levi Framingham from before the accident, on it and the word *Longbow* in the stylized font from the original album.

Rob felt a horrible sinking feeling in his stomach, probably shared by most of his friends. It was as if his whole planned scam had just been chucked out the window in one go.

7

FINN WAS AMAZED HOW LITTLE THE MAN LOOKED LIKE his old publicity stills, but that was probably to be expected, as badly as Longbow had been injured in the middle of his tour for that first album.

Flipped a ground vehicle and tumbled it. Safety harness failed when the vehicle got t-boned by a heavy truck. Year plus in a hospital after they reconstructed his facial bones as well as they could from pictures and hope. And taught him how to walk and talk again.

It was no wonder Framingham had never released a second album, since it was something like five years before he could play the guitar again that well, and the galaxy had passed him by to the next up-coming star.

"Welcome," Finn exclaimed to the group, taking their measure as he tried to figure out what the hell was really going on here.

Didn't feel like an elaborate setup for an assassination. Why would you employ people so high profile? These sorts of things were generally done quietly. And if you were going to make a production of such a thing, why stop with just this small team.

Finn could see Queen Jessica, or more likely David the Regent, sending a team of ninjas, if it came to that. Technically, they would be in their rights, as he might not have sent in more than a nominal sum in tax revenue over the last three years, calculating his distance to the capital against the values of the mines and the geographic location of *6940 Draconis* in the scheme of things.

Nobody would normally drop a colony here, except that the *6940 Draconis* system itself was in something of a salient, a thumb that stuck into a pocket, with *Salonnia* on one side and *Lincolnshire* on the other. Nifty, if you wanted to occasionally smuggle things to higher yielding markets without necessarily declaring them. Or paying the right taxes.

And hey, there's pirates here. I'm sorry but your cargo got taken at gunpoint. It was insured, right?

Finn smiled as he shook hands and let muscles in those grasps telegraph physiological notes to him.

Jorge Royo had not changed in eighteen years. Maybe forty, if you went back to early publicity stills, from the days when he was a serious actor. Before that one swashbuckler romantic comedy exploded and made him the biggest comedic actor in the octant for a few years.

And the man still possessed the most perfect sun tan ever recorded, according to experts who tracked that sort of thing.

His handshake was firm, but still a touch soft. Not quite as dominant as the eyes might have suggested.

Mrs. Jones was…

How do you describe the most beautiful woman in the galaxy?

Blond hair brushed back and full. Piercing blue eyes that

seemed to hold the slightest hint of sadness to them. Cheekbones that might have been cut with a chisel.

Physically, the woman had passed the first bloom of perfect youth. It was there in the skin on her wrists and neck. Mid-forties, he would have guessed, depending on the work done, but she was still all curves and seduction, with muscles that suggested hours in the gym every week and a lot of time on a treadmill in space.

Finn kissed her hand gallantly. How often did you meet true royalty in the flesh?

And Longbow.

It really was him, although you had to kind of squint. Not that Finn could imagine why they would impersonate the man, since almost nobody remembered who he was, anymore. Which was a damned pity.

The next man was a flunky. Tall redhead with freckles and the beginning of a paunch. Bowed legs that made his walk awkward and a little silly. Smelled of chemicals Finn couldn't identify, but it wasn't aftershave. At least he didn't think the smell qualified as aftershave for most of the women he had ever met.

Finn wasn't going to judge.

The last man was a grifter. That much was obvious. A man with a dozen scams running at once, like irons in a fire that he could pull out as he needed. Or as the mark tumbled onto some bit of truth and needed to be distracted.

Yes, the grifter, Segura, would simply tack onto a different heading as the winds changed, flattering and threatening subtly as needed.

Finn smiled at the man anyway. Worse came to worst, he could probably just have the man shot out of hand. That was one of the perks of being governor of an entire planet. You could do shit like that as long as you didn't ruffle too many feathers.

"How was your journey?" Finn asked as he got everyone seated, him at one end and Steafan on the other, with Aoki across from Mrs. Jones and the men scattered around that. Jorge Royo and the grifter ended up at his end of the table.

"Excellent," Jorge chimed in, reaching out and grabbing a martini glass, then sipping delightedly at the contents. Even here the man was famous. "So nice to be remembered."

"Remembered, señior?" Finn asked. "I would think you were quite famous still."

Jorge shrugged in a way that communicated a level of angst that never made it to his eyes, a secret well hidden.

"You would think," the god of tanning acknowledged, and then gestured at Finn's shirt. "But even here, Framingham has more fans that I,"

"Luck of the dice, Señior Royo," Finn tried to take the sting out of things with his smile. "My daughter found his album and played it constantly when it came this far. Eventually I got infected, as my wife can no doubt testify."

"Do you have others in you?" Aoki turned to Longbow with a mock-serious face. "It's nice, but I'd like other songs to listen to, and he will not be moved by modern music."

Longbow shrugged diffidently, and then seemed to reach down into himself to find the words.

"I never could do lyrics, ma'am," he replied in a voice so quiet Finn had to read his lips from seven feet away. "Learning to play the guitar again took so long that I never pursued it. The residuals do well enough, even now, and I can occasionally find work doing soundtracks to take vacations."

Finn perked up. He hadn't realized that there was other music the man had done.

"What films have you worked on, Longbow?" Finn called politely, hoping not to scare the man back into his shell.

"*Twilight at Arkos Seven*," the rocker mumbled. "*The*

Servant's Destruction. A few others. I mostly did the arranging and the strings."

Finn nodded to Steafan. His First Officer nodded back, obviously fighting not to roll his eyes at the unspoken orders to locate those soundtracks and acquire them. Finn's musical tastes were only sort of a running joke in the palace.

House servants began to deliver trays at this point to a buffet table along a side wall. Mimosas and such for everyone but Jorge. Both continental and hot options, depending on tastes and culture.

Finn had been awake since ungodly early, as had the others, if they were coming into orbit. Probably ship's night for them, but omelets and various sausages, plus all manner of fruit from the greenhouse dome and freshly baked pastries.

Conversation was mostly interrupted as the two women went first, and then all the men, with Finn waiting until last.

The group was somehow more subdued than he anticipated. He had been expecting some level of boisterousness, especially remembering the debaucheries Jorge Royo and his uncle had gotten into back on *Callumnia* that one time.

This almost felt like a wake, a brave face on a depth of sadness.

Finn waited until the food was done and the plates cleared, noting who had refrained from alcohol this morning, going after coffee instead.

"So I understand from my First Officer that you're interested in trying to make a movie," Finn addressed himself to the grifter. Watched the sman perk right up and prepare a spiel. "Has my office gotten a copy of the script to review? And your proposals for tax abatements and local service contracts?"

Nice way to deflect the man. Cool his ardor. Good scams

always wanted to hit hard and fast and then run away before you figured out you'd been had.

Not quite the same way most pirates did it, but Finn had always had better success with quiet things. Disappeared ships instead of captured or wrecked ones. Smuggling things in impossible ways and never getting caught.

Even hiring his old ship, *Dragonfly*, as an armed convoy escort, where he could use his expertise to outthink the other captains, and make one hell of a profit for a much lower risk exposure.

The grifter deflated, just the weeest bit.

"They have not," he replied, a little off kilter already. "I was unaware that was a protocol."

"Assuming you wish to explore tax breaks and local contractors, that sort of legalism gets routed through my office," Finn smiled triumphantly. "Much easier to weed out the bad customers that way, so we can deal with legitimate businessmen such as yourself."

Finn had to give the grifter credit. The kid managed to not flinch all that much. So maybe there really was a script. And it was good enough to convince Jorge Royo and Mrs. Jones to attach themselves to it.

She had been a fantastic action star, up until a few years ago. Amazing stunts married with first-rate acting chops. Maybe she missed that, turning into the mother in romantic comedies or the betrayed wife to some action star male?

But maybe they were both suddenly out of work and desperate, she and Royo? Had the dream factory suddenly awakened and moved on to younger, cheaper stars, still disposable enough?

"I will have a copy transmitted as soon as we get back to the ship," Segura nodded, suddenly more of a chastened schoolboy and less of a pimp. "Obviously, we could only guess at what the protocols might be in *Corynthe*, Governor."

"Thank you," Finn acknowledged. Best to get it all out on the table now, so he didn't waste time if it was all a scam. Steafan could smell those things out pretty quickly. "So why the impatience?"

Royo spoke up suddenly, his voice taking on some of the grand eloquence for which he had been known throughout his career.

"Two issues, really," the man's bombast came back with a fist slammed emphatically on the table, yet still turned down to just the right level for this small of a room. "That bastard Gutierrez got a sniff at this script and hired a hack to make a different enough copy of it that I can't sue him. Plus, he's got an in with some folks in *Salonnia* to help him make it. Shooting on location, you know. More expensive than a soundstage, but when you can borrow ships and crew, your overhead drops tremendously. I want to beat him to the punch. Plus, his crew are going to be impersonating pirates, but I wanted the real thing."

"I see," Finn replied noncommittally.

"If your uncle was still alive, I'd hire him," Jorge waxed poetic. "Got a small role that would have been perfect for him."

"Oh, he's still alive," Finn smiled. "He retired five years ago to a beach on *Petron.*"

"*Petron*?" Jorge sudden turned his attention and his rage on the grifter. "Damn it, Segura, why aren't we on *Petron* doing this?"

It was instructive, watching the kid placate Jorge without ever giving anything away. Or losing control of his lunch ticket.

"They've gone legit there these days, Jorge," the man said carefully, like he was talking to an angry bull. "Almost as bad as *Ramsey* for permits and regulations. Filming would take even longer than if we'd stayed home in *Lincolnshire* to do this. You want real pirates, right? Not past-their-prime poseurs living on old glory."

Oh, that was a low blow, kid. Rub his nose in it just a touch, without slapping him in the process.

"Jorge, we said we'd do it Rob's way," Mrs. Jones spoke with a plaintive edge just barely detectable. "You need to let him work."

Jorge's rage collapsed into itself and he leaned back, grumbling mostly under his breath and taking a hard hit of martini. More than Finn would have liked to drink, even in friendly company.

"And you, Mrs. Jones," Aoki asked to keep the conversation flowing. "I read somewhere that you were going to pursue more serious roles in the future."

"Where it turns out I can play the supportive wife of a man up for awards," Mrs. Jones suddenly had a cruel sneer to her voice. "Or the nagging mother bothering the flavor of the week sex kitten. There are villain roles, if I wanted to chew scenery. That's about all *Lincolnshire* cinema offers a woman over thirty-five, madam. Let me go back to kicking ass and taking names."

Finn flinched inwardly at the tone. This woman was still a goddess, and she had to be in her early forties at least. The polar opposite of Aoki, blond hair to black. Muscles to warm curves. Blue eyes to brown. But she was still distilled sex in a bottle. Steafan had been covertly staring at her low-cut top, hoping nobody noticed.

But Finn had been doing the same.

The scam made more sense now. The kid had a script. Or, more likely, Jorge had a script and the kid had gotten himself attached like a tick, driving things to get financing and permissions for a slice that probably wouldn't be that much, but would establish him as a player later, especially if

Royo and Jones owed him favors for resuscitating their careers.

Longbow was the odd man out, but if he was reduced to doing soundtracks these days to pay bills, he was probably also looking for a good enough payday to break back into the big leagues.

Finn wondered how he could cut the kid out and manage the rest. And if it was worth doing.

8

Rob collapsed into the booth back aboard *Valencia del Oro* with a mug of coffee in his hand and the beginnings of a fantastic headache. The others had followed him in still silent after the debacle of a meal with a man too sharp for their mission.

"Kid, kid, kid," Jorge settled in beside him with a fresh martini. "You were great back there. Don't let anyone tell your different."

Rob fixed him with a disbelieving eye, but Roxy smiled at him. Longbow practically preened. Nigel muttered something about cooking back in the machine lab and vanished.

Raef just sat in the middle of the booth and watched things.

"On the brighter side, I don't have to sex kitten all over the place," Roxy laughed. "I might have nothing to do on this gig but lay by the pool and complete with Jorge for tan."

"Don't be too sure about that young lady," Jorge growled. "I'm sure there's still a decent level of seduction in your future."

"You saw that way the man looked at his wife, Jorge," Roxy grinned. "Longbow's more likely to succeed at seducing the governor than I am."

"Ah, but you forgot about the other man, sweetie," Jorge grinned back. "The one who spent the whole time trying to look down your front and study your breasts."

"Jorge, most men do that as automatically as breathing," she sighed theatrically and settled back. "I could dress like a nun and they'd be trying to catch a peek at my ankles."

"They are nice ankles," Longbow observed. "Especially when you…"

"I didn't ask you, Levi," she growled.

Rob settled his weight forward again and studied the group.

"You think he's not onto us?" Rob asked. Mostly Jorge, but everyone. Raef grinned innocently, but she hadn't been there.

"Oh, he's absolutely onto us, kid," Jorge said. "But you showed him all the wrong things. Or right, depending on where you sit. Poor guy thinks we're all saps and that you've got us strung out on a merry song and dance routine, and that you're looking to leapfrog our fame and contacts and get rich."

"I could get rich in this business?" Rob asked innocently.

"Only when you go freelance, Handsome," Jorge smiled. "That club where we meet? I own the joint. As well as about a dozen others in various cities. Great way to generate cash flow, then launder it when the Service pays me under the table for things. Like this mission."

"Okay, so how do we spin this scam to fit things?" Rob fired back. "Assuming we can keep running these lies and not get caught."

"Well, like Roxy said, Longbow gets to play the ingénue now," Jorge laughed as Levi leaned forward and did a melodrama waif facing eviction for her father's bills. "That's pretty good. You sure you were never an actor?"

"Oh, I could have been an actor," Levi reminded him. "But I wound up here."

"We got a middle-aged fanboy," Jorge continued. "That line about you needing someone to write lyrics is probably blossoming as we speak. I'm guessing someone is off to find you a writer. If that works we might also end up with producer credits on Longbow's long awaited comeback album, if that's what it takes to get the governor on board."

"Hey, Raef," Longbow turned to the captain next to him and kissed her on the cheek. "Can I hire you for a year if I need to do a concert tour?"

"Only if the Service is paying for it, rocker boy," Raef laughed. "You're too cheap."

"Madam, you wound me," Levi played the displaced lover.

"She's right, Levi," Roxy laughed. "You are cheap."

"I prefer to think of it as frugal, I'll have you know."

"Whatever, kid," Jorge took charge again. "So, Handsome, here's where it gets a little strange, but you're absolutely the best agent I know for it."

"Go ahead," Rob said seriously.

Jorge didn't say things like that frivolously. The man was a legend because he was the best, and only worked with the best.

"So Finn probably thinks you're the weak link here," Jorge said, falling into a rare serious moment. "He'll be looking to rescue the three of us from your clutches, which is about what we expected, but he'll be doing it through Longbow, rather than Mrs. Jones. My game won't change much, so I get to drink and carouse on someone else's creditstik, which is still the best game in the world when you can get it."

"Okay, so we keep playing it straight, as far as he's concerned," Rob agreed. "Then what?"

"At some point, he's going to have you utterly outmaneuvered because he's such an awesome operator," Jorge grinned. "That's when you'll drop the boom on him. By then we should have a pretty good idea which way he'll jump, and Roxy will have been plying her talents on junior varsity players to bring them to the table, as will I."

"The man had a hard, cold look in his eyes, Jorge," Rob reminded the man.

"He did," Jorge agreed. "Try not to get yourself arrested or shot before you can have that showdown scene, okay? If he didn't react like he would, I would be talking about cutting him completely out as a worthless sack of shit, like that commodore we captured with the ship. Only the good guys are going to go out of their way to help us do this thing."

"So we feel better by cheating a paladin than a rogue?" Rob asked, clarifying.

"Oh, he'll get something out of the deal," Jorge said. "Not sure what just yet. Maybe a new Longbow album and we'll ask him to sing backup on a track or something. That's Levi's scam to sort out. We just back him when we get there. Remember, the Governor is just a gatekeeper, not the whole mission. You and Nigel will be doing the heavy lifting from here, just like last time."

Rob nodded. He wasn't a wide-eyed innocent any more, if he had ever been. And at the end of the day, his orders were to find a way to neutralize a secret naval base that a Salonnian Syndicate had built. The kind of base that threatened trade in peace, and gave them a nasty edge for surprise raids, if war ever returned to this sector of space.

The latter was harder to guess, since *Corynthe* was supposedly tightly allied to both *Aquitaine* and *Salonnia*'s patron, *The Fribourg Empire*, at least today. Hell, peace might be breaking out all over the octant as everyone turned together to face down some distant, robotic, killing machine closer in to the center of the galaxy.

Of course, that was when the mice were most likely to get up to mischief. Look at Handsome Rob, for instance.

And at the end of the day, Rob was a patriot. He just had a weird way of expressing it. Looking around the table he nodded to the rest of them. They all had weird ways of being patriotic.

But *Corynthe* was still technically the enemy. Anything that weakened a rogue Governor, even a nice one, helped secure *Lincolnshire's* future, if this Queen Jessica could turn *Corynthe* into a legitimate threat to *Salonnia*.

"So I have one get-out-of-jail-free card here?" Rob asked, doing the math in his head.

"Probably two," Jorge's seriousness was back. "If you play the first one right, you won't have to blow your cover until later, but let's assume that our first mistake is critical, if not terminal to this mission. You set to play the patsy, kid?"

Rob grinned.

"You mean I stopped, with you people?"

Roxy leaned close enough to punch him in the shoulder, but there was no force behind it. He really did belong with this team now.

Which was good. He was going to have to swindle an entire planet of cutthroat pirates next. While not getting caught.

9

FINN DIDN'T LIKE THE AMBITIOUS LOOK IN AOKI'S EYES when they got back to their suite. He had about an hour until he had to go into a an entire afternoon of meetings, but he could still play a little hooky with his wife. She just didn't look like she wanted to fool around.

"You think he's serious?" she asked absently.

"Which conversation are we having?" Finn grinned at the woman.

"Huh? Oh. Longbow," she finally got him on the right page of the hymnal. "Could a second album be as easy as finding the right songwriter?"

Finn shrugged. He knew next to nothing about how music worked, other than you hit the play button and sat back to enjoy it.

"You aren't already scheming how to find him one?" she turned to him with some level of surprise, however mock and contrived it was.

They had been married more than thirty years.

"Do we think he wants one?" Finn shot back.

"What do you mean?" her gorgeous brows knit together.

"Maybe he's afraid to try it again, dear," Finn said, taking a spot on the couch and patting the seat. She settled in and leaned against him. "Think about fighter pilots who go through that level of trauma and manage to survive. How many of them ever really make it back to flying?"

"You think he can't face it?" she asked, eyes pensive.

"I think it has been over twenty years, Aoki," Finn said. "And the original album made enough money that someone would have tried, before now. Probably, he had a shitty contract and didn't feel like going through all that again. That might be why he does soundtracks. Someone left a hole in the legalese, and that gives him an out."

"So we shouldn't try?" Aoki asked.

"We shouldn't necessarily expect to succeed, which isn't the same thing," Finn said.

"True," she agreed. "Plus, you'd have to go through that pimp in the shiny suit to do anything."

"Him I'm not worried about," Finn grinned. "I'll just throw him in jail if he gets pissy. But I need to handle that task delicately, at least for now."

"Why is that?" Aoki asked. "When have you ever had to walk on eggshells with a foreigner?"

"It's not him," Finn said. "I need to see what kind of hold he has on the others. What kind of control he has. They obviously trust him to get this movie thing made, so just cutting that punk off at the knees might ruin everything that they were trying to accomplish."

"You might help him anyway?" she was a little aghast, but she was a school teacher by training, not a politician. Even if she hadn't been in a classroom in a decade.

"Maybe," Finn admitted. "Maybe not. For now, I'm just going to watch him. Or rather, Steafan is. If he steps over a line, then I'll throw him in jail."

Finn's comm rang before she could reply. Checking the readout, it was Steafan.

"Got news?" Finn asked as he answered.

"Maybe," his First Officer replied. "Those folks delivered a copy of the script. An actual, paper printout marked DO NOT COPY. I have someone reading it. We might have a problem."

"Okay?" Finn said. "What kind of problem?"

"It's pretty good, from what they tell me."

10

THIS WAS A LITTLE MORE LIKE IT. HANDSOME ROB looked around the dive and counted noses as he made his way to the bar and grabbed an empty bar stool at one end.

It was weird being in *Corynthe*. Not this dive, particularly. He had been in hundreds just like it on dozens of planets in his previous jobs as a courier and field agent. No, the gender breakdown was off, at least subconsciously.

Any other place, on any other planet, it would probably be two to one males over females. Not a true reflection of the sort of gender equality you found in ship's officers, because a lot of women didn't necessarily hang out in joints like this. But they were around.

Here, there were no female officers in sight. No, scratch that. Two. Maybe. Two more that Rob would have qualified as wives if pressed. Five others had the look of professional escorts about them.

Yeah, only two women in here looked like they came off a starship.

It had been a decade since that *Aquitaine* captain, Keller, had stolen the throne of *Corynthe*, killing a massive block of folks who didn't think a woman had the balls to do something like that. Women were freer to pursue naval careers. Rob even knew that a few had succeeded, but they were far between.

To see two in here surprised him. He presumed they were from out of town or something.

At least he was dressed not to stand out quite so badly as professional women did, as he looked around and ordered a beer.

There seemed to be a uniform look among the men so desperately not-belonging to an organized military. Rob grinned. All alike in their non-conformity, as his mom used to say.

Tall boots that buckled on the sides, usually either metallic silver of some shade or a hardened plastic shell, mostly black. A few had old-style leather boots once called cavalry.

Tight pants that tucked into the boots. Again, usually black, or at least a very dark shade, not counting the one guy in the corner with neon yellow boots and hot pink pants.

There was always one.

The planet above was a desert, but they were underground here, and temperature rarely moved by more than a few degrees. Ships were pretty much the same temperature at all times, except when you dialed your cabin down to sleep.

Pullover shirts, generally tight enough usually to show off muscles, in some stretchy, jersey-like material. And there were muscles. Queen Jessica might have generally outlawed dueling as a thing, but these men had gotten to be officers and captains by knife fighting, most of the time. You had to be big and fast, or small and even faster to survive and thrive.

The shirts were where their personality showed. Colors. Patterns. Images or logos printed on the front. Long sleeve or short or medium. Nothing Rob could see there qualified as a *uniform*. Heavens forbid. Hot pink pants were paired with a burgundy shirt that actually had white lace at the collar in a way that managed to look almost regal, rather than silly.

Score points for hiring a good tailor.

About half the men were wearing an outer shell of some sort, be it a light jacket, a dressy vest buttoned up, or a light vest open like a jacket. Here, the men came back to conservative colors, usually monochrome. Over the burgundy shirt, the one man was wearing a white vest, almost skin tight like a corset, done with green paisley patterns.

Loud, but somehow not obnoxious. Perhaps stylish at a level nobody else in the room was capable of understanding, let along achieving. He would stand out anywhere except perhaps *Anameleck Prime*, the industrial and financial capital of *Aquitaine* that also billed itself as a fashion capital.

It helped that seated with him was one of the two women in here that looked like officers rather than hookers or office girls looking for a meal ticket. Rob made eye contact with the garishly-colorful captain while sipping his beer, tilting his head in a way that hopefully communicated a desire to talk without necessarily interrupting. He didn't mean to accidentally be making a pass at the man. The mission didn't call for that. Yet.

One eyebrow, almost delicately chipped out of stone, went up as the man stared back, perhaps taking Rob's measure as Rob had his. A quick nod of assent. A murmur to his companion, who glanced back and shifted her chair around a bit to watch the room better.

It probably wasn't accidental that the captain was in the corner, facing out.

As Rob approached, he studied the man himself. Most of *Corynthe* was made up of two, dominant genotypes that had managed to blend well over the millennia, especially as you got closer to the capital world of *Petron*. Northern Europeans and Japanese had been the two ethnicities one found most commonly, this far out on the fringes of the galaxy.

The captain was a blend Rob had never encountered before. Like his clothing, it worked, while being utterly unique. The man's skin was somewhere between the dark brown of the African Diaspora, somehow mixed evenly with the golden tones of *Nihon*, the parent colony that sent so many children further out. Bronze was as good a color as Rob could find to describe the man.

His face had hard planes to it, which reinforced the association. Clean shaven. Curly hair that wasn't the tight rings of his African ancestors, kept short enough that nobody could easily grab a handful in a fight. Brown eyes alive with intelligence and humor.

The woman with to him was dressed like the rest of the men. Steel plates and buckles on black leather boots. Black pants cut just baggy enough that they didn't call attention to her legs. Mustard cream shirt, again a little loose. Shell jacket in medium gray.

What stood out was how short the woman appeared, but also how broad. Maybe five feet tall, from what he remembered when she walked in, depending on her boots, but shoulders like many of the men in here, broad and muscular. Thighs like she lifted massive weights on a hip sled every morning.

Her face was neither homely nor comely. Broad and flat in a way that suggested Chinese Diaspora, but red-gold hair cut to a short length just a little longer than a buzz. She didn't smile, but didn't scowl angrily at him either.

Rob counted the whole as a win. He had only come in here to scout things so that later they could get serious about casting. But this might be too good to pass up.

The noise level in here was a dull, throbbing murmur, but there was no music trying to compete, so people could talk without yelling.

"Roberto Segura," he introduced himself as he got close. "May I?"

The captain nodded and gestured to the spare seat, himself in the wrap-around corner of the booth.

Up close, the man was armed, but so was everyone in here. Belt knives, telescoping batons, and pistols, depending. You had to be deadly committed to start trouble in a joint like this, so probably nobody ever did.

"Okonkwo Nakano," the man replied with a pleasant-enough smile as Rob sat. "Captain of *Wild Duck*. You are not from around here."

"What makes you say that?" Rob asked.

With his free hand, Nakano gestured to Rob's outfit.

"Not the height of piratical fashion," he said with laughter in his eyes.

Rob looked down and considered. No, probably not, but he wasn't trying to fit in here. His job was to stand out, rather like bait, and see who nibbled.

Laced up ankle boots in rough, brown leather, tied in white. Gray knee socks with a red stripe on white at the top. Pale, gray flannel knickerbocker pants. Not even the Plus-Fours that were making the rounds again. Darker gray jacket with several external pockets, two slit and two patch, as if he was going shooting and needed a place for his shells. White, dressy shirt that buttoned up with a foldover collar containing a blue tie rather loosely knotted. Collar on the jacket up.

With the middle button on his jacket as the only one fastened, he was the model of stylish, fashionable gentleman on *Ramsey*. Here, he just communicated wealthy foreigner in conscious and unconscious ways.

As was his goal.

"No," Rob agreed. "Not from around here. *Lincolnshire*."

"Indeed." Nakano mused. "My Tactical Officer, Lilijana Kozel."

She just nodded, the hard, silent type.

Rob was already halfway in love with her as a character for the movie, even before she spoke.

"Charmed, madam," Rob nodded.

She didn't hold out a hand to shake, so he didn't either. He suspected that the woman defied most gender stereotypes consciously, as she dealt with pilots and crew who might only now be coming around to the future, if at all. Rob would have guessed her in her mid-twenties, maybe about a decade and a half younger than her captain.

"What brings you to *6940 Draconis*, Segura?" the man asked. His accent was hard to place, and his eyes were attentive and bright in a way that Rob wasn't fooled by.

The man was still a pirate captain in a pirate realm.

"I'm making a movie," Rob grinned as both of them grew a little hesitant and confused.

"A movie?" Nakano echoed the words, as though perhaps he was a cow digesting his cud. "What kind?"

"It's kind of a pirate romance," Rob offered. "With a healthy dose of betrayal, comedy, and action sequences, both on the ground and in space."

"I see," Nakano replied in a vague, almost bland tone. "Well, you may have come to the right place to do your research."

"Oh, we're past research at this point," Rob brightened. "Had a meeting yesterday with the Governor about permits and financing and such to film as much of it as possible around here. Right now, I'm in casting mode. Looking for local flavor. We could have done this back on *Ramsey*, but

Jorge wanted real pirates. Men and women who lived the life, rather than actors trying to somehow look tough."

"Casting," Nakano repeated distantly.

Kozel brightened from her general glower and leaned forward just a hint.

"Don't let him fool you, Segura," she explained in a smooth, alto voice that the sound systems would just love. "He is the very model of a modern major general."

Bronze could blush. Flush a little, anyway. Eyes dilated.

"Hush," Nakano ordered without much authority.

Rob grinned at the woman. He didn't understand the reference, but it was obviously something theatrical he could look up when he got back to the ship. Probably Jorge would know it off the top of his head.

Jorge was like that.

"Okonkwo, you were made for the screen," Kozel grinned along with Rob.

"Actually, I'd like to talk to both of you," Rob said.

It was her turn to blush now, at least briefly, before she turned bone white.

"Oops," Nakano grinned. "And here I was, hoping you were looking to smuggle something interesting in or out of *Lincolnshire* space and needing an expert."

"That might also be on the menu," Rob offered vaguely. "Jorge's looking for as much realism as we can afford, so that might involve some action sequences with real guns fired at mock up targets."

"Jorge?" the woman seemed more interested in the show biz side of things than her captain did. Or at least than he let one.

"Jorge Royo, the actor," Rob said matter of factly. "Executive Producer, Director, Star. Mrs. Jones is also along on this one for one last, big thriller while she still can."

Rob liked the way the woman's face grew intent. She

turned to her captain and some invisible, silent conversation went back and forth that Rob couldn't really parse.

"We have a schedule," Nakano finally said aloud.

"Bergier has a schedule," Kozel corrected him. "What's it hurt if they don't end up getting chased on a run? Especially if we don't tell them and they panic anyway."

Some of Rob's confusion must have showed.

"A *Salonnian* operation," Nakano explained. "We have a retainer from one of their competitor, another of the Syndicates, to disrupt things as much as possible. Keeps my pilots sharp and the crew fed and happy."

"What's your ship?" Rob asked, suddenly deep into Field Agent mode. Hopefully, invisibly.

"*Wild Duck*?" Nakano inquired. "A 3-Ring Mothership of the older school. Like you, far from home."

"Older school?" Rob followed up.

"King David is building newer, heavier 4-Ring ships these days, and standardizing both the hulls and the flight wings. We're too far from the centers of power to get upgraded in my lifetime, plus, we don't really defer to *Petron* all that much."

3-Ring Mothership. Built something like a goose with a big head at one end and a big body at the other. Bridge forward, engines and most of the defensive firepower aft.

In between, literally three rings of smaller craft around that long neck, usually Starfighters, maybe with cargo containers and a tug, depending. According to *Lincolnshire* Naval Intelligence, as they had absolutely refused to shut up about while he was there, no two fighters were identical, except for the new, Royal squadrons. Mostly just rebuilt junkyard scrap with guns.

"So if we wanted to perhaps hire you and your ship for some things, you might be able to make space in your schedule?" Rob asked in that hopeful, lawyer voice.

"That would depend on the contract offered, Segura," Nakano replied, suddenly a hard captain on his deck again, and not just a fashion plate in a bar.

Two of them, with Lilijana Kozel. Rob was pretty sure you had to have your shit together and dangerous, if you wanted to stand out this much, compared to the other captains. And while a 3-Ring wasn't as dangerous as the bigger, 4-Ring monsters, it was still likely to be a capable vessel.

Rob nodded to them. He slipped a hand into one of his jacket pockets and pulled out a pair of business cards Raef had printed up for them, with local contact information. He made a point of including Kozel in the conversation.

"I would like to perhaps entertain the two of you in the near future," Rob said, rising to depart. "After I have had a chance to talk to the Governor and see where we stand with him, as well as some of the other captains, if you know any you might recommend. We're looking for naturally colorful characters that we can cast in minor roles and bit parts, as well as a few slots we're hoping for find among whatever professional or semi-pro acting talent there is. Please let me know if you have any questions?"

"I will," Nakano replied in a crisp, formal accent.

Rob finally placed the man's language. He was speaking English with an *Aquitaine* accent, which was highly unlikely out here. Not impossible, but long, long odds.

"You also aren't from around here, Captain?" Rob tried to set his tone as inquisitive without prying. "Judging by your accent?"

"Correct," the man nodded. "I was born on *Nahar*, which is about as far from the long *Salonnian* border with *Corynthe* as you can get, long ways around the galactic rim rather beyond even space *Corynthe* claims on their most ambitious days. Why do you ask?"

"Your accent is pure *Aquitaine*, sir," Rob smiled. "That would actually help in our filming, as they would be one of our targets for distribution."

"Well, I speak Igbo at home, Segura," Nakano replied. "As does about half of my crew. The other half, including Kozel here, are more local."

"Lucky for me then that we met thus, Sri," Rob nodded back. "We'd like a colorful movie filled with interesting people. Hopefully we can make something work."

"Indeed," Nakano grew formal. "Good day, then."

"See you soon," Kozel smiled at him as well before he departed. It seemed more than just normally friendly.

Rob left the rest of his beer on the bar and put an extra tip with it. Word about him would get around, as those two talked, and others asked Nakano what had just happened, so he wanted the bartenders and staff to have a good opinion of him, next time he came in here fishing.

Things were already looking good, as long as he could convince a bunch of pirates to go do violence to complete strangers for money.

He didn't think it would be a difficult task, convincing them. But they were pirates.

Anything might go.

11

————

"WHERE IS EVERYONE?" ROB ASKED AS HE ENTERED THE ship's lounge.

Dinner time usually meant that the room would be filled with the smells of food, but it was just Raef in here, wolfing down a bowl of udon and reading something on a smallscreen device.

"Jorge happened," she looked up and paused. "Got everyone rooms at a hotel in town and moved himself, Roxy, and Longbow over. You and Nigel have rooms as well, but neither of you were back yet to tell."

"You don't want a room?" Rob asked, kind of knowing the answer already, but wanting to hear it from her directly.

"I prefer my ship, Rob," she replied flatly. "I'll join you occasionally for meals and meetings, but I sleep better in my cabin, on my bed, listening to my ship's sounds, with the temperature just the way I like it. Plus, I don't trust pirates any further than I can throw them."

"So us gone is…?"

"Almost my idea of paradise, as long as I can log into the

69

local news and entertainment network, Handsome," she did smile this time.

"Okay, well I've started making contact with some local ships," Rob smiled back at her. "Would you be the person to ask about reputations and all that?"

"Probably," Raef replied. "Not that I'm likely to know much, this far from home, but better than anyone else on the crew. Not sure who you could get an honest answer from among the locals. Who's first?"

"*Wild Duck*," Rob answered. "A 3-ring mothership."

"Captained by Nakano," she completed the sentence. "A little more high profile than most ships in this section of the galactic arm."

"That's the man," Rob agreed. "Said he had a retainer contract to hassle a Syndicate named Bergier, on behalf of some other Syndicate. I presume it's another case of plausible deniability."

"Probably," Raef nodded grimly. "What do you need to know?"

"Anything and everything you can lay hands on, Raef," Rob said. "At some point, if we make a movie, he's on my list of people to cast. If we go beyond that into serious business, I'd like to be able to judge the military and political intelligence we get from him or the Governor against what you know. Won't save us a double-cross, but might warn us what kind would be coming."

"It's *Corynthe*, Handsome," her face had turned sour. "They're already calculating several steps past a triple-cross, more likely than not."

"Yeah, but I got Jorge on my side," Rob laughed cruelly. "They'll all be in for a surprise."

"You hope. That it?"

She picked up her noodle bow expectantly, so Rob took a

cue. She and Nigel were the quiet ones of the group. He could give her some peace.

If everything worked the way Jorge had planned it, she would literally be in the middle of the craziness when the trouble started.

12

───────

Finn noticed that Steafan had added a late
meeting today, but left the details blank. Probably not a bad
sign, since Steafan hadn't barged in on other meetings to
interrupt with some world-ending event.

Still, it was later than he usually worked, so he sent Aoki
a note and got an auto-reply.

Huh. Must be girl's night out or something and he'd
forgotten.

At least that meant he wouldn't get in trouble for coming
home too late for dinner.

Steafan entered a few minutes later, with Aoki in tow.

"Am I having an intervention?" he asked, only half
joking.

"Not yet," Aoki smiled sweetly. "Anything you felt the
need to confess?"

"My wife's almost as much of a goof as I am?" Finn tried
to read her smile, but she was playing her cards close.

"Almost," she came around his desk and kissed him while
Steafan took a chair.

Aoki ended up on the couch, more or less splayed across

it like she was expecting a fashion photographer to happen by. Weirder things had happened. Finn sat at his desk and waited for them to get to whatever they were up to.

"So you asked about the thing that apparently happened with Jorge Royo a year ago in *Salonnia*," Steafan began, pulling out several folders from a briefcase Finn had missed when the two entered.

"And?" Finn asked.

"It's messy, boss," Steafan said. "They were all set to make a movie, but got sidetracked because Longbow was supposed to be playing this massive concert. Fifty thousand sailors, give or take, were getting there and getting organized. Near as anybody can tell, the commodore of the naval base decided to defect, stealing the largest warship in the entire *Salonnian* Navy owned by any of the Syndicates and flying it to *Lincolnshire*, where he immediately claims asylum, turns State's Evidence, and was given a new life, disappearing from history as near as we can tell into a new identity nobody has since cracked."

"Seriously?" Finn found himself leaned forward with his hands flat on his desk.

"Like I said. Total, freaking mess," Steafan shrugged. "Jorge and his friends did not end up getting their movie made, and pretty much disappeared back into everyday life until they show up here with a completely different movie script, this one even better than the last. One presumes that maybe the government of *Lincolnshire* paid them some sort of kill fee, but no banks or financiers would touch the place."

"Same players?" Finn asked.

"Jorge Royo, Mrs. Jones, and Longbow, yes," Steafan replied, checking his notes. "*Salonnia*'s not talking much. Even less than normal, so that's about all we know without activating some of our sleepers for confirmation, but I don't think this is that important. Those three have worked together for the better part of fifteen years, if Longbow did some of the soundtracks he mentioned. And before you ask, no, I haven't found copies of them yet. You may have to send a courier to *Lincolnshire* proper to buy them."

"Okay, so why have you finagled my wife into this meeting, Steafan?" Finn changed the topic.

"She brought me, boss," Steafan shrugged. "I'll let her explain."

Finn knew his dear wife was up to no good by the way her eyes sparkled. And that soft, almost innocent sigh that escaped her lips. Fat chance he'd fall for such projected innocence. He'd been madly in love with this woman for the better part of thirty years. He knew her games.

"Out with it," Finn commanded, with about as much authority over the woman as she might allow him to have.

"So there are a few songwriters in this town," she smiled demurely. "Friends of friends of friends, sort of thing."

"Uh huh."

"And I might have asked around," Aoki continued, circling her prey like a cat.

"As one might," Finn agreed.

One did not press Aoki. Not successfully, anyway.

"If they were to make a movie on *Draconis*, or in the area, one would presume that Longbow might need a full studio in the city proper to work," Aoki continued. "There are a few, one of which is owned by a friend of a friend who is also a lyricist with a few local hits."

Finn grunted. Local music tended towards the purely electronic, as well as frequently airy and random.

He had always wondered what would happen if he hooked a synthesizer up to a navigation computer and plotted a multi-stop course from here to *Petron*, and then routed the output into music. Popular music today might sound close to that. Just about the opposite of Levi

Framingham's music, any way you wanted to slice it, but it might be a carrot they could dangle in front of the guitarist.

Like they were dangling the carrot in front of a governor right now?

"And?" Finn finally asked, when he realized she had stopped talking and was just smiling at him.

"So we don't know what happened last year," Steafan spoke up. "Maybe completely innocent. Maybe the world's perfect scam. Maybe they were enlisted to help the man defect. Maybe they were just innocent hostages."

"I'm still not seeing the crisis that has you two sitting in my office playing word games," Finn pressed a little harder now.

"So perhaps," Aoki took up the thread. "Just perhaps, we could arrange things to get Longbow isolated from the others if we offered up our help with soundtracks and maybe a second album. Someone might be able to get more useful information from the man, if the other two weren't around. Or that lawyer. They seem to be the big fish, and Longbow something of an afterthought. An old friend you'd help out when he was down on his luck."

"You think we might buy some of his friendship?" Finn asked flatly.

Hilariously, they both shrugged almost identically. Close enough that Finn laughed, and caused them both to blush.

"Can't hurt to ask, boss," Steafan said. "There is money in the Arts budget this year we could move around. Plus, it would qualify as an investment, if an album comes out of it, so maybe income later. Maybe more if there's a legitimate movie here, and not just a scam being run by that suit, Segora."

"What do we know about the kid?" Finn felt his face harden.

"Nothing. Not without finding someone from *Ramsey*,"

Steafan said. "Too far away, unless I dispatch a boat, which I haven't done. You expect them to be here long enough that we could round trip a spy request? Probably six months, best guess."

"Send it anyway with the next ship making a run into *Ramsey*," Finn decided. "If they're on the beam, we'll still be talking in six months. If it's all a scam, he'll probably have blown town by then, leaving the others here holding the bag."

"Do we find some preliminary financing that maybe gets the movie stuff in motion?" Steafan asked. "That anchors them to the ground pretty hard, especially if we do it in dribbles, rather than making that guy's eyes light up with greed."

"Six months is more than enough time for someone to also make it to *Petron* to tell David what we're up to," Finn acknowledged. "And for him to come back with a squadron, wanting their cut. Plus all the back taxes we haven't been sending in. Which is where the Arts budget comes from."

"Are we at a dead end?" Aoki asked.

She wasn't on the government payroll directly, but she and Steafan were still his two closest advisors. The only two he trusted not to leak to someone.

"No, but keep an eye on who Segura and the others talk to among the Captains," Finn said. "That will tell us a lot about how serious they are."

Steafan's belly laugh sounded rather ominous.

"Good news then," the man said. "*Wild Duck* was just about the first person he talked to."

"Nakano?" Finn laughed. "Well, they were serious about local color. Do they know the man's a *Salonnian* spy?"

Steafan shrugged rather eloquently. Aoki's was less so, but just as relevant.

Too many unknowns. Was this all just a complicated,

Salonnian plot to take him out? Wouldn't take much to make enough Captains restive that they decided that maybe he needed to be replaced as Governor of *6940 Draconis*.

Bizarre way to do it, but it would certainly leave someone with white hands, afterwards.

"Watch them like hawks," Finn ordered the man. "Longbow, too, but approach him unofficially about your cousin the lyricist."

"My cousin?" Aoki asked.

"Everyone in this system is your cousin, dear," Finn smiled at her. "I learned that a long time ago."

She grinned back. Those contacts were what made her dangerous. But he could trust her.

Because her head would be on the chopping block right along with his, if this was all a trap.

13

"So what do we know, kid?"

Rob looked up as Jorge finally emerged from his bedroom, into the rest of the presidential suite he had been sharing with Roxy. Longbow had a smaller suite down the hall, and he and Nigel were down a few floors with the plebes.

Not an entirely bad way to live, given the housing and entertainment budget the Service had come up with for this mission.

"Just going over the plans for the set we'll be building for act three of the movie," Rob felt his face go sour. "Is anybody that stupid? Are we missing something important in the defenses? Is this really believable?"

He gestured to the big, paper printout in front of him, done like blueprints for an Art Department to build. But it was, near as he could tell, a dead solid copy of the architectural as-builts of the place.

Jorge wandered close, white, terrycloth robe tied loosely and a martini glass in one hand.

Seriously, as far as Rob knew, the best way to torture the

man wasn't to withhold alcohol, so much as take away his martini glass and make him drink tequila or something.

Jorge sipped now and made appreciative noises as he studied the map.

"So you were in the navy kid, right?" Jorge glanced up at him. "Before all the rest of your life."

"I was," Rob replied simply.

Nigel hadn't found any listening devices in his regular, thorough sweeps of the place, but that didn't mean they weren't there.

"So the Navy in every nation is a government operation, Handsome," Jorge smiled. "With very strict acceptance criteria around hardware and facilities, because mistakes mean people get killed, and politicians get angry calls from relatives of the deceased."

"Yeah, that jibes with what I remember," Rob said. "It's been almost a decade."

"Right, but this is *Salonnia* who are playing the bad guys in act three," Jorge circles the table to get a better view and get the morning sun out of his eyes. Well, noonday sun. Jorge didn't do mornings, unless he was still up. "They aren't a government. Instead, you have somewhere between eight and eleven criminal Syndicates in charge, depending on things. Some of them like each other well enough to cooperate. Others would see the planet burn, just to take a rival down a notch. And we need realism here, rather than silly notions. That's what sells this film to the audience."

"Right, but one gun station, off to one side of the base?" Handsome put his finger down on a single tower, located well away from the main part of the *Secret Salonnian Naval Base*. "That's not enough."

"Oh, I agree with you one hundred percent, kid," Jorge laughed. "But this is actually fairly standard for *Salonnia*, and based on a real place. Remember, this is a business operation, not a government. More guns means more expensive, so they did a cost/benefit analysis and calculated risk curves. There are two big guns in that tower, and that gives them just enough redundancy to check a box on a list. And it puts all those folks clear across the landing field from the big shots, so they can come and go in their fancy yachts without having to walk too far. Or in this case, ride, since we're on the surface of an airless moon."

"And nobody would be able to attack this?" Rob stood and began to pace.

Partly, he was playing for the galleries, assuming that someone was somehow listening, but partly this was out of inexperience on his part. And some level of disgust.

An *Aquitaine* heavy cruiser with an escort of some sort could have just sailed right up to that base and probably pummeled it into the lunar dust. Or maybe stood well off and launched a wall of missiles at the place.

Lincolnshire didn't have any vessels with that sort of firepower. Even the ship he helped Jorge steal last year would have been outclassed, but that was all the little notes about gunships on the ground. Where Jorge's finger landed now.

"They would not, kid," Jorge noted. "Because in addition to the guns, there's normally a defensive squadron of fighters at a place like this. As for the script, we've added a raiding squadron. Pocket gunships with short-range jump that lets them sail for a week or so to hit someone and then either capture ships or blow things up and return. That's the genesis of the script, that need for a team to disable the base before the cavalry rides in at the last minute and saves the day."

"So you and Mrs. Jones and a team hit the place and basically shut it down?" Rob asked. "Easy as that?"

"Handsome, it's never as easy as that," Jorge laughed. "You look at pages eighty to one oh five, give or take, and you'll see how messy it gets as we try things, fail, try more things, fail again, and then the boss monster has us trapped and we're about to die. Really looking forward to the guitar solo that Longbow comes up with as we peak at that climax. He's really good at that sort of thing."

"Well, I've got you some names," Rob pulled out his pocket notebook, and honest-to-Creator paper and pencil thing he kept in his jacket to jot down notes like a real producer. "Five or six captains, including three Motherships, all the way up to a 3-Ring. I know the script calls for a 4-Ring, but there are only like ten or twelve of those in *Corynthe*, these days, and almost all of them are either based out of *Petron* or make regular runs there."

"We can fix that part in the filming," Jorge decided. "The script was a little generic on that one, because we leave that to the Art Department when they make sets and costumes. Tell me about *Wild Duck*."

"Did a little research, and she's a weird mix of raider and freighter," Rob replied. "Seventeen slots with five gunship raiders like the script has on the surface, so he's outnumbered there by seven. Eight Starfighters, so again outnumbered, but only by two. A dedicated cargo tug and three slots that normally haul standard, *Aquitaine*-style shipping containers. Captain Nakano and his Tactical Officer, Lilijana Kozel are the most colorful folks I've talked to."

"Who did you say he worked for?" Jorge asked

"Don't know as yet," Rob said. "Kozel mentioned that they were on retainer to hassle an outfit known as Bergier. Who's owns the base in the script?"

"Not Bergier," Jorge said. "I'd have to go back and look, because it's too early in the morning right now. Lemme work some magic on the man, maybe with Mrs. Jones, to see if we can get him to change sides long enough for filming. Or at least have a second contract."

"Kozel seemed interested, so she might be an ally," Rob

said. "Oh, what does it mean: *the very model of a modern major general?*"

He liked the way Jorge laughed. Deep and full, from his belly. That might be the first time he had ever seen that level of honest happiness out of the man.

"It's an ancient theater reference kid," Jorge finally managed after he stopped giggling. "A pre-starflight musical. Who said it?"

"Kozel, talking about Nakano, if I understood things," Rob answered.

"Okay, I gotta meet her now," Jorge said. "She's one of us, even if she doesn't know it yet."

"No seducing her without a contract, Jorge," Rob chided the man with a grin. "After she signs up as part of the production you can charm her all you want."

"Hey, kid, you know me," Jorge tried to play wounded, but couldn't keep a straight face.

"You can get all the girlfriends you want around here, Jorge," Rob snarked. "I want her in the cast. When you meet her, you'll understand."

"Fine," Jorge grumbled. "Set up a meeting. A public meeting over dinner, I suppose. Wouldn't want the wrong tongues to wag."

Rob laughed. Jorge wandered to the window looked out, pausing to glance at Roxy's open bedroom door.

"Where's she?"

"Down at the pool, working on her tan," Rob answered.

"Ya know, I shouldn't let her get within a light year of catching up," Jorge noted. "And it's probably a good thing we're all underground here. She's got no tan lines, so that would be one hell of a scandal, if she was outdoors. I presume tanning booths?"

"You got it," Rob said. "Stack of tokens on your nightstand."

"Okay, let me know if you need to find a slot in my busy schedule." Jorge turned and walked back towards his room. "Otherwise, keep up the good work, kid."

Rob nodded at the man's back, and then he was alone, studying his blueprints.

Filming the inside scenes around here wouldn't be all that bad. It was attack on a hostile base that would require a better Director of Photography.

Rob wondered what kind of hazard pay they would have to offer someone to do it.

Just how crazy were pirates?

14

———

Even more than twenty years later, Levi felt like a fraud signing copies of that old album. The one with a picture of an eighteen-year-old Levi Framingham under the word Longbow. He was long since past being that kid. But he still signed it for fans, like the Governor of this planet apparently was.

Hell, he didn't even look all that much like that kid anymore, after they had had to basically rebuild his cheekbones and jaw from old pictures. And Levi wore long-sleeve shirts most of the time. Light, so he could keep them pulled all the way down to his wrists. That hid most of the scars from the surgery that had rebuilt both of his hands.

He held his hands up now and looked at them, alone in this car of the tram after two people had exited at the last stop. Five years until he could play his signature song again with the passion and intensity he had had the first time he recorded it.

Five years in hospitals and rehab facilities, while his managers and company had bled him more or less dry with those crappy contracts and massive expenses.

At least he came out of it with a second career. Or third, depending on how you wanted to look at it. Too much time in hospitals, so he had gone ahead and gotten fully certified as an Emergency Medical Intensive Care Technician. A paramedic, had he wanted to go down that path.

He still did regular duty schedules to keep his certifications active. And ride-alongs, where nobody but a few even knew who he was.

Jorge and Roxy kept him sane. Sane enough, anyway. Combat medic on a team of…Levi supposed they were all spies, if you wanted to get technical about it. Secret Agents? Mercenaries? Vigilantes, considering the sorts of situations when the Service called them in to do things.

But he got to play guitar, and help people, and occasionally blow shit up, so life was pretty good.

"Now approaching Edo Block," a woman's pleasant voice filled the car. "Exit the car to the right."

Levi rose and grabbed his case from under the seat. That, a gun, and his medkit, and he could pretty much go anywhere in the galaxy on ten minutes notice.

The platform was empty, except for the Governor's wife. Aoki.

Tall in that way that Nihon descended colonies did, so roughly his height. Brown eyes that didn't miss anything, however innocent and distracted she might play. Curvy and maybe four or five kilos heavier than when she'd been at eighteen, but still attractive. The way her black hair was just starting to streak into grays gave her a sexy librarian thing Levi approved of.

Hopefully, he wasn't supposed to allow this woman to literally seduce him on this mission. Not that she wasn't a babe, but her husband was five miles of trouble all by himself.

"Good morning," she smiled at him as he emerged, apparently the only person for this station of the subway.

Her opening hug was just a shade beyond professional, but Levi had a guitar case, so he could make it awkward enough and step back with an innocent smile.

"So I understand you might have found some recording space?" Levi framed things in a professional setting.

He could still get all the innocent groupies he wanted, just by playing a couple of local bars. The power of rock and roll. No need to get into trouble with the Governor's wife.

At least until the mission parameters changed.

"This way," she hooked her arm in his, on the side opposite the case, and led him down a corridor.

This planet was just weird. They had the subway that went everywhere, but it was actually dug pretty deep, and all the buildings still went up, closer to the surface, rather than running just belowground and you went deeper when you got to your destination.

But they were underground, and that was good. He worked best on a semi-lit stage, or a quiet studio, without a lot of light.

Mrs. Fukui took him into a random-looking place with a big foyer. Over to the right and into a handy elevator. This one was glass on most sides, overlooking the foyer as a vertical vault, so each floor was actually more of a mezzanine as they climbed.

Cool. Weird, but still interesting. Plants everywhere, but that was to be expected. The locals were apparently treating this place like a space station, just one that was underground.

Fifth floor. If his math was right, they were actually just below ground here, with airlock-like doors that you could use to get out onto the dusty, reddish surface, if you had a reason to.

Down a hall, she rang a bell and a door buzzed, so she pushed it and they entered.

Levi might have just died and gone to heaven. Or hell, if the devil really was into rock and roll, like his dad had always warned him.

Guitars and basses on two walls. At least a dozen of each. Couple of drum sets. Keyboards. Other instruments, depending on your needs.

Whatever your needs.

Tall, spare skeleton of a woman rose from a table in the corner and studied them as they approached. Dusky skin way darker than Levi's or Aoki's, but not all the way down to African Diaspora. Long hair pulled back out of her face.

She wasn't homely, but nothing you'd write home about. More or less regular features with brown eyes and a hint of cheekbones.

"Longbow, huh?" she stuck out a hand to shake, which also broke Levi free from Aoki's grasp.

"That's right," he said.

"Aoki says you got all sorts of needs?"

"Maybe," he shrugged. "I'm supposed to be doing a soundtrack to a movie, but they haven't even started filming yet, so I've got no rough cuts, or even dailies to work from. Just a script and folks I've worked with before."

"We can always jam while you're waiting," the tall woman offered.

"We could," Longbow offered. "What do you play?"

"Everything," she grinned at him. "What do you need?"

"Studio band, if we're going to jam," he challenged her. "I'll assume you've heard my one album. I'd like to test some people out, so maybe I'll be able to have a full kit behind me and play a few gigs around town."

"Ten songs is a pretty short set," the woman observed. "What else can we play?"

Levi turned to Aoki, just in time to catch her face turn to innocent surprise, but he wasn't fooled. It smelled like a setup, but the good kind.

"I heard a rumor about a lyricist looking for some help," Levi said, taking in the long woman's demeanor. "Maybe we could throw in some classics with our jams, on our way to looking at working up some new songs?"

Might as well throw the gauntlet down right now. These people were apparently willing to fall all over themselves to seduce him. He could be seduced with music.

And maybe tall, gawky musicians, if she was any good. The woman smiled now and that seemed to change her entire being, from angry punk to musician. Lit up the whole room.

"I might have some things then," she said, holding out her hand again. "Naomi."

"Levi" he smiled back at her. "Let's you and me go jam for a while while we sort things out?"

She turned towards an inner doorway and stretched those long legs.

Levi turned to Aoki with a conspiratorial grin.

"Don't you tell anyone until we're ready to either record them or play a gig in public," he ordered her with a smile.

"Wouldn't dream of it," she answered.

Levi figured she'd be writing up full reports on everything for her husband, but that was fine. He was the Trojan horse on this mission, which was just silly. Usually, it was Jorge or Roxy.

Now he just had to work up the enthusiasm to actually record a second album, after a couple of decades of excuses.

15

Rob had arranged things to be a little low key, but still interesting. Quick buffet dinner for about thirty folks, back at the hotel where he was staying, with a lot of standing around, a polite string quartet, and lots of gossip.

Nigel was off doing god-knows what aboard the ship, allowing Raef the time to come into town without worrying about someone breaking in and doing anything. Longbow had more or less moved downtown, staying out for days and apparently crashing on someone's couch, like he was a broke teenager again.

So Rob was entertaining. Well, technically Jorge and Mrs. Jones were having a meet and greet with potential investors and interested parties, but that just meant he was responsible for all the technical details with the hotel and the caterers. The job of a producer, when you got right down to it.

The Governor was here, along with his wife and his First Officer. Nakano and Kozel off *Wild Duck*, currently getting ready to go do something in a few days, but everyone was being very tight-lipped. A few bankers. A handful of shipping magnates, what there was at least on a planet this small. They were all pretty small fry, as things like that went, but the cover story was good enough to bring them in.

Only one other captain had made the cut with Rob so far, of the three dozen folks he had chatted up. Probably could end up using half a dozen, but so many of them were almost interchangeable visually as characters, at least from a physical standpoint.

Rodderick Kedzierski, however, was not beige, in any sense of the word. He had long, curly hair with auburn at the ends and a mask of gray underneath as it had finally decided that the season was autumn. He was tall and lanky, having a little height on the Governor, but weighed probably what Rob did.

But the man was hard. Tough. Mean looking, whether you met him in a bar or on the street. Those stony, gray eyes peered out at you from a face covered with scars and tattoos he had accumulated in crashes, fights, and drunker dares. Rumor said they pretty much covered his whole body, proving just how lucky and tough the man was.

A few semi-friends had shared stories of the man's past. The several marriages that never lasted. The challenges when people though he wasn't charismatic enough to hold his place in the pack hierarchy.

Kedzierski smiled at Rob as he entered the room. The man was dressed in that standard, black uniform the Captains went for, just about the opposite of what Nakano wore every day, making the two of them anchor both ends of the spectrum for colorful fashion tonight.

If this was a really a casting call, Rob would have found an acting coach to teach Kedzierski how to handle all the details needed to make him the villain of the piece. The man just exuded badass all over the place like pheromones. And yet his ship, *Queen of the Borders* wasn't a combat craft, at least as the pirates would have rated it.

She was a 1-Ring mothership, but really the vessel was a massively overgunned cargo transport, even for around here. Her ring was three armed tugs, like pocket gunships rather than Starfighters, and three cargo boxes. As near as Rob could tell, the three Type-3 beams and six Type-1 beams she had as firepower rated her as the second most dangerous hull out there, behind only the new *Kali-ma* class 4-Rings that the queen of *Corynthe* was building in *Aquitaine* yards. Even *Wild Duck* wasn't as tough a ship, but she had a flight wing that made up for it.

Queen of the Borders was a porcupine flying in deep space. Best left alone, if you had the sense the Creator gave a goose. Not that many pirates had understood that at first, but there'd been enough bloody noses given out, in orbit as well as in bars, that Kedzierski and the *Queen* got a wide berth today.

"Captain," Rob made a point of walking over the greet the man. "Welcome and glad you could make it."

Kedzierski didn't look as thought he felt out of place, but many of the bankers and businessmen in the room looked askance at him. Might as well let them know that the man was a favored guest. Knowing Jorge, he was up to something, having explicitly included the man on the invite list.

Kedzierski nodded and shook his hand, but he wasn't necessarily one for small talk, so Rob aimed him at the buffet and the open bar with a smile.

Rob smelled Roxy drift up behind him. There weren't that many women in the room, and none of them had that perfume except her.

"It's fun," she murmured as she stepped to his side and turned him to watch the crowd circulating. "Not often you see Jorge bounce off a woman so badly."

It was not. More interestingly, it was Kozel that was proving impenetrable.

Jorge was being his charming self. Captain Nakano was certainly charmed and laughing at some story, but Lilijana Kozel looked almost bored.

Briefly, Rob wondered if she even liked boys. That might explain things. Except she saw him watching and her eyes lit up. She quickly backed a step to extract herself from the conversation with the men with a polite excuse and walked this way.

"Oh, dear," Roxy chuckled. "Jorge will never forgive you."

Before he could say anything, Mrs. Jones stepped away and expertly caught herself up with a group of ladies representing the local theater scene, some from the university and another who had a semi-pro troupe. That left Rob standing alone by the front door.

And Lilijana Kozel was making a bee line for him.

She still gave Rob the impression of a tall woman who had been squished a foot, with all the extra mass pulled sideways. She had shoulders and hips and thighs, but a narrow waist and nice chest. And yes, she could do more weights on a hip sled or bench than he could. Hell, Roxy was the only person Rob knew who might give Kozel competition in the gym.

She had a glass of something mostly empty as she stepped close.

"I need more," she held it out like a bouquet of flowers, smiling up at him.

Almost daring him to do or say something. Rob was used to women finding him attractive, but Kozel had not given off those waves before tonight.

Maybe it was because he was an outsider, and therefore safe if she wanted to fool around? Woman like that could never have a fling with a crewmember and keep her place. She'd have to beat them all up at that point. Probably could, if pressed. Best to remember that.

But yeah, Jorge had bounced right off.

"We should do something about that immediately," Rob took the glass from her hand and made his way to the bar.

Because Rob was the one paying the bills, the bartender reached under the counter and poured him two glasses of the good whiskey. Neat and room temperature, as was the only way to imbibe something so smooth.

Somehow, Rob found himself in a quiet corner of the room with her. Jorge and Roxy and the Governor apparently had things nailed down, when he glanced quickly at the room.

"I've been meaning to ask your captain," Rob said. "Since you're here, I'll try you."

"Is that what you had in mind?" she grinned up at him. "Trying me?"

Rob smiled and gave her a quick tilt of the head, as if to ask silently.

"Maybe," he offered carefully. "But here's my first question. I remember you saying you were bothering someone called Berger or something. That *Wild Duck* was being paid to, anyway. But who actually pays the bills?"

"Their name is Bergier," she corrected him absently. "And you'd have to ask Okonkwo on that one. Not my business to talk about."

"Understood," Rob nodded and sipped, as if thinking. "We've talked. Jorge and I have talked about maybe hiring the two of you, and maybe the ship itself to provide some really authentic flavor to things. Problem is, Bergier is a *Salonnian* Syndicate so Jorge's concerned that we might be getting into cross-border political issues we don't want to bite off."

"It's not exactly cross-border," she replied, sipping and shifting her weight in such a way that she was suddenly half-again closer than she had been.

Rob had to be careful not to breathe on her. Or spill if he took a sip without watching his elbow.

"Come again?" Rob asked.

"Maybe later," she smiled. "Not even there the first time yet."

Rob grinned down at her and the banter.

"I meant, how is it not cross-border?" Rob clarified.

"Oh, the people paying the retainer are another Syndicate," she murmured.

Rob noted that she didn't mention which one. Rumors floating around town had nailed it down to either *Black Aurora* or *Ahearn & Toledano*, but even the locals weren't sure.

Which might still be a problem, since it was the *Ahearn & Toledano* syndicate who had built themselves a secret base just across the border from *Lincolnshire*, from which they had engendered so much panic that the Service had offered up Handsome Rob as a ritual sacrifice.

So on the one hand, she might know that base really well. She might also be working for the very people Rob was trying to kill.

Not exactly the way to make small talk with a woman.

"So you aren't from *Corynthe*? *Wild Duck,* I mean? " Rob decided to play dumb.

His mom swore by the technique.

"Oh, we are," she chuckled. "Better, *Salonnian* money is flowing right into *6940 Draconis*, every time we order supplies or go drinking in bars."

"And the other captains don't get up in your face about it?" Rob let his voice grow to surprised, especially as she had shifted again and they were pretty much dancing while holding highball glasses at this point.

"The first rule of *Corynthe* is mind your own business, Segura," she growled in a playful voice. "Or should I call you Handsome Rob, like Royo does?"

"What would delight you, Lilijana?" Rob decided to push back.

Just a little. See if this was a setup or just an invitation for a casual romp.

"If you're a good boy, I might show you later," she purred now. "But I wasn't done. Second rule, *Wild Duck* can take anybody else in the area, if push comes to shove. We've got the heaviest flight wing and the best pilots around. You'd have to go to one of the 4-Rings at *Petron* to find better fliers."

"So you're a woman who can just take anything that catches her eye?" Rob dangled the bait out there.

Not even delicately.

"We're pirates around here, Handsome," she leered at him in the same way he had probably done to women he had encountered.

Most of those women couldn't knock him down and hold him against his will, though.

"I shall keep that in mind, Lilijana," Rob leaned back just enough to allow some daylight between them. "For the next two hours, I'm required to be on stage for these people. After that…?"

She leaned back as well. Sucked down a hard smell of his aftershave, which was the same one Jorge used.

I mean, if you're going to learn, learn from the best.

It was interesting watching her pupils dilate, just a little, as she sipped some more of that really excellent whiskey.

She turned first, taking a step away, then turning back to

fix him with a look that promised he had only escaped her for a little while.

"We'll see," she murmured back over her shoulder.

Rob caught his breath and moved counterclockwise to the woman as she walked away, just so he could mingle with some of the guests. A few had noted the interaction. Many of them apparently approved.

Or Lilijana Kozel frightened them, which was always a possibility.

They *had* come out here to recruit some pirates to do something piratical.

But he might be in trouble if *Wild Duck* was working for the bad guys.

16

───────

Levi checked the clock on the amp as the last notes of the song faded. Getting close to dawn, if he had the latitude and season correct in his head. Stone cold sober didn't make up for utterly freaking exhausted.

But damn, this felt good.

Naomi had quietly put out the call for some help to jam and record. The result had been a handful of her friends in the industry. In eight hours, they had learned one new track well enough that this last run through had been with the machine recording.

A beep filled the room, indicating that the recorder was off and they didn't have to remain silent any more.

"Vishnu, that was smooth," Dutch said from behind his standing, electric bass. "Two or four slot on the album?"

Longbow shrugged. Organizing the tracks was the job of the producer, a petite blond named Alicia on the other side of the glass who had piped in some of her own backing vocals, along with Naomi on rhythm guitar.

"Aiming for two right now, Dutch," Alicia replied over

99

the intercom. "We'll do number one tomorrow night, if everyone's free to do this again."

"Count me in," Wolfgar stood up from behind a drum set so large it sat on a rotating platform with an motor that could spin it in place.

"Got a gig with some other folks tonight," Pepe said as he closed his keyboards. "Gimme a couple of hours and I'll send over a tape of the synths before I rack out. You want track three or five if I'm on a roll?"

"Five then three," Alecia opened the door and joined them in the main recording studio. "I'm thinking we've got nine or ten songs that should make the cut, depending on solos, intros, and orchestral overdubs I'll work out later. In a hard week, maybe ten days, we ought to have a rough cut you can use as a set for live gigs, with an eye towards rerecording everything in a month for a final album. Plan accordingly."

Levi noted that she hadn't asked anyone if that schedule worked for them. Just announced it to the group and apparently expected them to make whatever adjustments they needed to do, like Pepe clearing his other band, or bands.

There was an assumption that everyone in here played regular gigs with at least one other band. Four in the case of Wolfgar, but good drummers were usually worth their weight in whatever medium of exchange you wanted to offer.

It felt good to Levi, though. Everyone here was roughly his age at the youngest, up to Dutch, who looked older than the moon overhead. But they had all come in like pros. Learned their bits after only a couple of passes through, then ran their expertise over the simple things he and Naomi had showed them.

It wasn't as good as the *Longbow* album, but this was one night jamming and recording with complete strangers. Idly,

Levi wondered if they should delay the real mission long enough to actually finish recording. He'd worked with a number of recording techs in his time, and Alicia was in the top three all time.

He might actually generate a followup to *Longbow* that would sell maybe half as many copies, which was impressive, considering how heavy that first album had dropped.

Fast enough, everyone was gone, leaving him, his guitar, and Naomi. Somewhere, the sun might be rising soon.

"I can't figure you, man," she said, still facing him from across the circle with that cherry red guitar in her lap. "Most people would either be all in right now, or just humoring me with a polite pat on the head. You're somewhere in the middle."

"Honestly?" he unplugged and rested his guitar on a rack, standing and stretching as he did so.

"Yeah," she fired back, mirroring him. "Honestly."

"I keep expecting to wake up and all this will be gone," Levi replied, gesturing to the room around them. "Poof. Not the first time I've been in a studio trying to record a follow-up to *Longbow*. All of them fell apart at some critical juncture, right when it might have worked."

"So we should grab this while we have the chance?" she asked in a voice with traces of something under it he couldn't name.

Levi turned and found her suddenly closer than she had been. Not touching, but not that far from it either.

"It'll be gone like morning dew," he said simply. "Nothing to ever show we were here."

For a moment, her eyes got a faraway look, like she was about to kiss him. Levi had wondered which of them would make the first move. They had danced around it for a week, never talking, but it had been there in the back of her eyes, so he stood perfectly still, mirroring her.

Her lips moved, like she was talking to herself, but no words came out. Like she was standing in an empty stadium. After a moment, he shrugged and stepped towards the refrigerator to grab a beer.

She was still standing perfectly still when he twisted the top off the bottle, a statue carved in chocolate opal. Levi wondered if he had turned into some sort of medusa accidentally and had turned her to stone.

Something in the woman clicked, like lightning. She turned and strode to the front room on a mission. Levi followed. There, he found her at her desk, scribbling furiously in the notebook where she wrote her songs, so Levi went back and grabbed a second beer, resting it nearby on the desk, but she was oblivious to him.

He found a chair and sat, watching the woman commit art in her own world like he was a ghost or something. It was interesting. He didn't do lyrics, but if you handed him some, and if they worked, he could hear the music under them almost immediately.

She surfaced after about five minutes of writing, thinking, and fidgeting.

"You're still here," she observed absently, like that was a surprise.

"We're all ghosts if you aren't looking," Levi replied.

He wasn't sure where those words came from, but once spoken, her eyes got huge and she started writing again, diving headfirst back into the notebook.

Poof. Gone.

Levi finished his beer and studied the instruments on the room. Almost every kind of string you could play, along with a few woodwinds and some brass. Every culture he could think of and several that eluded him completely, unless that one was a contrabrass clarinet.

"Sorry," her voice brought him back to the present. "Something you said. Things you said."

"Gathered that," Levi smiled. "Want to share?"

She surprised him by standing, walking over with the notebook in hand, then more or less draping herself across his lap. Writing that must have been an even more exciting experience for her than it had appeared from over here.

Levi read the words. Heard the rhythm underneath. The breathing.

Notes appeared in his head. He looked around, almost frantic.

"What do you need?" she asked, not moving.

"Guitar," he said.

She probably didn't realize he was strong enough to do it until he actually stood up, lifting her, and carried her back into the studio, like crossing a honeymoon threshold. Down she went onto her stool.

Levi grabbed his axe and plugged it back in. Closing his eyes, he read the words aloud in his head, plucking. Somewhere in the back of his mind, something compared how oblivious he was to the outside world right now with where she had been five minutes ago.

A second pass, with notes plucked as he spoke the words aloud. Yes, there.

Third pass, he changed the key down a note. This was a power ballad, it needed to be slower and deeper than the rockers.

Fourth pass, he was actually playing the song now when the bass line suddenly intruded into his conscience. Naomi setting the backbeat.

Yes. Later, keyboards and maybe a whole string section, but right now, just raw, stripped completely down to the two of them.

"From the top," Levi said absently, utterly lost in the magic of music making.

The last notes faded.

"And cut," Naomi said, breaking the spell of concentration that had fallen over him.

"You recorded that?" Levi asked, looking up for the first time in however long.

"Oh, yeah," she said. "I absolutely wasn't missing that."

She stood and racked her bass. Walked over and racked his guitar. Straddled his lap on the stool and wrapped her arms and legs around him.

"Now you're going to take me home and bang my brains out, understand?" she explained as she kissed him.

"Yes," Levi agreed, breathless.

He stood, with a spider wrapped around him, and carefully made his way to the front room. She unwrapped herself but kept hold of a hand as the shut the lights and locked the hatch.

Walking away, Levi knew that there was a pretty good chance the version Naomi had just recorded might be the one song on the mythical album that maybe never got made, if Jorge took the whole planet sideways with his madcap mission.

But he might also need to sneak back here and finish it. That nameless song probably had as much power as the original *Longbow* did.

Pity they might put a price on his head before he finished recording it.

17

Rob leaned back with his coffee mug in one hand and smiled at the afternoon sunlight streaming in from the patio. Life was good.

Longbow seemed to agree. They toasted silently with coffee mugs as the others filtered in from elsewhere.

"Vishnu, do I end up looking like that?" Jorge asked the room as he sat at the head of the table with a martini glass in hand. "After a night of excellence?"

"Like those two?" Roxy asked. "Yes. Frequently. But both those boys look like they got their coals thoroughly raked last night. Am I right?"

Rob just smiled at her. Felt Longbow do the same.

"Jorge, you're like that all the time," Roxy interjected. "Good for you to see what the rest of us have to suffer through."

Jorge harrumphed sourly, but didn't offer any more commentary. His exploits in the bedroom were legion and legendary.

"Nigel, where are we?" Jorge asked instead as the cowboy made his way into the room.

Rob noted that the dude was carrying some sort of personal-scale scanner today, one that played both white noise and quiet, instrumental music in the background as he walked all the way around the room. The doors were all closed, but the curtains were open.

It was weird, being on the top floor of a tall building that only stuck one story above ground. At least triple-thick windows kept the temperature nominal in here.

"So far, so good," Nigel replied. "No bugs. You bribed the maid with enough money and threats that nobody has been able to outbid her."

"Yeah, but that's likely to change when we get down to end-game," Jorge snapped. "Calculations change."

"Are we?" Roxy asked. "Getting to end-game?"

"Maybe," Jorge sipped at his endless martini and watched Rob and Levi with near-disgust on his face, mixed with grudging jealousy. "Had long talks with both of the captains Handsome invited last night. Got some of what I needed to know from Nakano. Handsome, did you managed to gain any useful intelligence while you were interrogating that midget chick?"

"She's not a midget, Jorge," Rob smiled serenely at the man. "Might be able to outlift Mrs. Jones, if we wanted to stage a competition. She had needs, and I provided a useful outlet."

"No, I did not want to hear the gory details," Jorge growled. "Yes or no?"

"She won't confirm anything except Bergier, but I got the impression that *Black Aurora* was more likely the Syndicate than *Ahearn & Toledanoi*," Rob answered. "They've managed to keep that secret from everyone around here."

"Yes," Jorge agreed. "Nakano danced around the topic as well. I'd hate to try to hire the man to attack his own base. Not even pirates are usually that crazy. But we're also not under the gun for time here, like we were before. Longbow, where are you at with our overarching distraction?"

Rob liked the way Levi's eyes lit up. He wasn't sure he'd seen the man actually happy. Like, ever. Always either totally locked in on his mission, or melancholy about things he never mentioned.

Today, the man positively glowed. Rob wondered if the two of them might blind everyone else. Again, the quick toast with coffee mugs, celebrating that everything was all right in the world.

Then Levi dropped the *bon homie* like a blanket and turned into someone else. This was the character Rob remembered. Intensely focused. Lethal.

It was like holding a razor-sharp longsword in your hands.

"The Governor's wife? Aoki Fukui? She's deadly serious," Longbow said. "They've cranked the seduction up to eleven on this one, although I'm as surprised as the rest of you that I'm the target. She came through with a studio, a recording engineer I'd like to kidnap and take home with me, and a lyricist who might make me famous again."

"Really?" Jorge leaned forward almost as quickly as Rob did. "Talk to me, son."

"Aoki Fukui knows my music through her husband," Longbow nodded. "Naomi writes some powerful, good poetry that just seems to play music to me when I read it."

"So we're kinda all in on a soundtrack?" Roxy asked.

"Worse," Longbow said. "Right now, I've got a writing partner, a backing band, and possibly enough music on hand to record a full album that might be almost as good as the first one. The producer, Alicia, wants us to do a set of gigs in a few weeks to tighten up the sound, and then record a dozen or so tracks so she can build it."

Jorge whistled.

"What happens if the mission screws that all up?" Rob asked.

"Got no contracts in place right now, but we'll need to do something about that soon," Longbow turned to face him. "We've got outtakes and bootlegs good enough to play on all the channels right now. That's how good these people play. I presume the money's coming from the Governor, so they'll own it, more or less, especially as pirates. I could see them walking this all the way into a comeback concert and tour to support a new album in six months, if we aren't careful."

"Man, Levi. You really do a wonder messing up my plans, don't you?" Jorge asked.

"Oh, I kind of enjoy it," Roxy offered, smiling like a Cheshire Cat. "How many times have I had to play the nymphomaniac with the locals to distract them? Rather enjoying my time with nothing to do but look beautiful and elegant. Maybe you should get off your ass and run a mission to blow something up?"

"Very funny, woman," Jorge refused to take the bait, but Rob and Longbow snorted in unison. "Nigel, how are we on blowing things up?"

"Invented a new steadycam for the mission," Nigel preened. Rob couldn't think of another term to describe the man's smile and attitude. "Looks like a standard over the shoulder model, but holds four, short-range, armor-piercing missiles you can program with the view-finder. Kill a small tank while still recording full track."

"You going meta on us?" Jorge asked. "Making a movie about making a movie?"

"Hey. I just build special effects stuff," Nigel shrugged and grinned. "If it all ends up on the cutting room floor, you'll have to take that up with the editor. Guy named Royo or something."

Jorge scowled as everyone else laughed.

"So do we do this with *Valencia* or *Queen of the Borders*?" Jorge asked the group. "Raef gives us better control of the whole, but it puts her and our getaway at risk. *Queen* is a much better cover story, but we introduce a wild card."

"If you can get Captain Kedzierski to go along with it," Rob corrected him.

"If, yes," Jorge said. "Think I have an in there. The man has a chip on his shoulder. Well, a number of them, but one I can exploit."

"And *Wild Duck*?" Roxy asked. "We'll blow everything wide open if you guess wrong. Then our cover is utterly ruined and the best we'll be able to hope for is that we can get gone before we get arrested or killed."

"Do we sound out the Governor and his people?" Rob asked. "They might have spies that know."

"Again, one mistake there an we're compromised seven ways to Sunday," Jorge said. "Plus, I don't want you burning your first Get Out Of Jail Free card on something this piddly."

"So we just need to know who *Wild Duck* works for?" Longbow asked. "This Captain Nakano?"

"That's right," Jorge replied. "Got an idea?"

Longbow shrugged and took a breath.

"Depending on how you want to look at it, I've already got a band, these days," the guitarist said. "And the possibility of a tour to dangle out there, as well as residuals from an album. Lemme dig into it from my end of things and see what comes up. You are forgetting how small this place really is. How isolated. Crap ton of people, sure, but they're all either underground or in the mines, down here. Plus a bunch in orbit on the various stations and factories and shipyards. My people might know."

"It frightens me, working with you folks," Jorge grinned.

"We've been here three weeks and you're already talking galactic tour. Mrs. Jones has a tan beginning to challenge mine, so I'll have to spend less time in meetings with bankers and more time in a booth."

"Maybe you should have them build a bigger booth?" Rob offered. "Like a sauna, but a tanning room for a group instead?"

"Kid, I like the way you think," Jorge said. "Have the hotel rig something up. I can have meetings and maintain the perfect tan. Have them either include a wetbar, or build it close to a bar so I don't have to walk far to seduce the girl behind the counter."

Rob muttered something ugly under his breath, but Jorge's orders fell under the rubric of producer. And it would have him in more regular touch with some of the folks in the engineering sections of this hotel, so more opportunity to expand his network, if he ever needed to come back to *6940 Draconis.*

"Anything else?" Jorge asked. "If not, you have your assignments. Rob, I want you to start casting for security forces next. Find me goons who know how to shoot."

Rob nodded as everyone rose. Lilijana would be heading to orbit by now, and not back for roughly two weeks, depending on whatever her ship was up to. It had been a hell of a sendoff, even if she turned out to be the bad guys by the time this was all done.

Now he needed to dig deeper into the underworld here and find himself some killers.

18

FINN HAD NOTED THAT HE HAD AN OFF-SCHEDULE meeting with Steafan, at his flat, rather than in the office. Usually that was the indication of something so high security that his First Officer didn't trust the people working for them in the trenches.

Unsure, he had a glass of wine on the side table and the bolter with the safety on in his hand when the knock came. Aoki was out doing something she had been vague about, so Finn wondered if Steafan had asked her to be elsewhere.

Finn rose and checked the screen showing the hallway outside his door. Steafan and another man, that one with a hood up shadowing his face. Nobody had weapons, so Finn unlocked the door and stepped back.

Steafan must have understood, because he triggered it open from his side and didn't move.

"Pizza delivery," he said conversationally.

"No mushrooms?" Finn fired back.

"Never," Steafan agreed and stepped forward.

As codes went, it was the sort of thing that made no sense to an outsider, but sounded like a joke, rather than a call/counter one or the other of them could use to indicate trouble.

Or none, in this case.

Finn went back to his seat and clicked the safety on his bolter. He did rest it next to him, within immediate grasp, but there was a stranger with Steafan.

The two of them entered finally, closing the door and stepping into the room. The stranger pulled his hood back to reveal a hard face. A little heavy, like he was carrying an extra ten kilos that was starting to turn to belly, but not there yet.

Steafan gestured the man into the other chair, across from Finn, and took a seat on the couch.

"I won't bother with names, just to protect everyone," Steafan began, his own voice low and dangerous. "Suffice it to say this man is one of mine, deep in the dark parts of the underground, and does not report to anyone but me, and only when he had news."

Finn nodded. Deep cover spy with a single comm number he could use if something happened and he needed to disappear, in order to testify later. That was how you survived in the rough and tumble politics of *Corynthe*.

If Steafan was willing to vouch for him, and bring him here, it must be good. And dangerous.

"Talk," Steafan ordered the man.

The stranger took an extra second to compose his thoughts. He had a look about him like an ex-cop. Maybe retired. Maybe gone mercenary. Maybe just kicked off the force for being dirty. It was hard to tell around here. Most cops weren't all that clean. They just understood who paid the bills and behaved accordingly.

Most of the time.

"There is a secondary network of folks with some level of military or paramilitary backgrounds," the man began, in a surprisingly high, tenor voice for as big as he was.

Finn nodded. He knew about those sorts of things. If you weren't a Starfighter pilot, you could get work as crew, with usually meant either highly-skilled engineer, or highly-dangerous goon.

This man didn't look like a machinist.

"According to the word on the street, some folks are looking for small arts and close combat experts," the soldier continued. "Cover story says they are casting for extras in a video shoot, but anybody showing up to inquire is put into one of the commercial Hogan's Alley combat simulators and given a minimum score they have to achieve in order to make it to the second round of interviews."

"What's the cutoff?" Finn asked carefully.

He hadn't been a pilot, either, so he had an excellent working knowledge of guns and tactical combat ranges.

"Better than someone wanting a spot on *Wild Duck* or one of the combat motherships," the man replied tightly, eyes locked on Finn's at an extra level of communications. "Out where you have to be a pretty seasoned combat vet to place. At Juney's place, they wanted an eight-ten or better. "

"Vishnu," Finn exclaimed.

That sort of number cut off about half the people hired as gunslingers on most ships.

"And someone else has to vouch for your combat experience," the man continued. "We're a small enough group around here, at least the ones not permanently attached to ships right now, that nobody could inject an imposter."

"Have they told you the mission?" Finn asked.

"Negative, sir," the man shook his head. "But they had Juney's set up for clearing a couple of semi-secured buildings. As in, blow a door with simulated high explosives and take out guards inside before they can kill you. "

"Eight-ten?" Finn repeated.

"Yes, sir," he said.

"Did he hire you?" Finn asked.

"Second highest score," the stranger finally smiled. "We're on retainer right now, just so we don't take any other gigs, but I got the impression that they plan to grab everyone and go somewhere with them in the near future. Isolate them, and then identify the target and go tactical. They've got good systems in place to give everyone exactly the minimum information necessary to take them to the next step, and nothing more."

"Are you compromised by being here?" Finn asked.

The stranger turned to Steafan rather than answer.

"I don't think so," his First Officer replied. "I have procedures in place for this sort of thing, and they seemed to work. That was what I needed you to hear, Finn, so I'd cut him loose now unless you have questions."

"None for you," Finn acknowledged the man.

"Very good, sir," he rose carefully, turned, and walked to the front door, letting himself out without another word.

Finn rose as well and locked the door, just in case, before he returned to his seat and put the bolter down.

"I've read that script," Finn said. "It does call for a small assault against a couple of buildings near a landing field, in order to disable communications and a weapons tower."

"Yes, but that's usually a series of close-ups with a lot of smoke and noise in the background," Steafan replied. "Maybe one or two shots showing a team of gunmen racing across the field to set it up. I'm given to understand that they have twenty to thirty men currently lined up. Just putting them onto a single crew as boarders would rank the crew among the most dangerous that docks here. And as a rule these men don't get along well enough to be on the same crew together for long, but they're professional enough to do a movie shoot. Or a single mission."

"That's what frightens me," Finn said. "I'm guessing you think they're maybe getting ready to take out a government building? Like, maybe ours?"

"It has a bad feeling, Finn." Steafan said. "I've listened to my gut and rarely been wrong."

"Are Royo or Jones involved, or just that pimp Segura?" Finn asked.

"So far, just him," the First Officer replied. "The rest are under enough surveillance that we doubt they're up to anything except living a nice life while someone else pays. Either Segura's money, the provenance of which is unknown, or local folks trying to buy goodwill and consideration when the big money does come through and those two make a movie. With or without our boy."

"And I'm beginning to lean that way, Steafan," Finn said. "Segura's starting to move out of dumb and pretty and starting to look like a threat."

"Do we take him out or bring him in?" Steafan's eyes got deadly serious.

"Bring him in," Finn decided. "Or rather, have him arrested and see what happens. We'll decide after we have him if he should die in a tragic misunderstanding in a jail block."

"On it."

Steafan rose and let himself out. Finn locked the door again and then grabbed his wine glass.

You did not become a Governor by being complacent. If Segura became a problem, he would be eliminated, easy as that. Finn was sure he could find other people to step in, if there really was a movie happening, but movies didn't need a platoon of top-notch killers.

Only revolutions did.

19

"Señior Segura?" a heavy, ugly voice intruded, to go with the shadows that had suddenly blocked out all the light coming from the rest of the bar.

Rob looked up and took their measure, trying to be perfectly still.

Four of them, holding shock wands openly. Uniforms. Badges on their chests. Ugliness on their faces.

Rob turned to the other person seated in the booth with him and gave the man a weak smile.

"I'll be in touch," he said simply.

The man was a little white around the edges right now, but he owned a catering company. The four newcomers promised violence.

"How may I help you gentlemen?" Rob asked carefully.

"We have a warrant for your arrest, Segura," the one in the middle said in the sort of casual tone that suggested they'd be happy if he resisted and they had to detour by the hospital on the way to the jail.

"I see," Rob said, still not moving. "On the inside of my jacket, under my left arm, is a pulse pistol. I'd rather not try to get it out for you, but I don't want any misunderstandings, gentlemen."

The boss leaned forward and tapped Rob on the hand with the shock wand, which proceeded to ground itself into his nervous system perfectly.

Rob figured he'd blacked out for a couple of seconds, because when he could see again, one of the cops was holding his pistol and they had lifted him bodily out of the booth, one man holding a wrist on each side.

"Anything else?" the man in charge asked.

"My wallet is on the right side, with all my paperwork," Rob struggled to keep his voice calm as he tried to get his feet to work. "But other than that I don't even have a pocket knife."

"That's good, Segura," the man said.

He found his wrists cuffed expertly, and then one of the men produced a hand scanner that gave him a solid once over. Nigel could have hidden things, if Rob and Jorge had thought he might need them, but even that would have probably given too much away right now.

Instead, he was led out the front of the bar, with one man in front and the other three behind. Running would do him no good, as the first one back there had his hand on the cuffs to control Rob.

He did make eye contact with the bartender, who nodded as they left. Rob never ran a tab in that place, but instead put money on account and kept it topped up, paying tips from ready cash as he went, just so they liked him.

Hopefully, that meant that the man would call Jorge as soon as the excitement died down. Not that Jorge could do much, unless it became necessary to take out the police station as part of his rescue, but that would blow this mission apart. Still, they had gamed it out and laid contingency plans.

Lincolnshire's navy could always petition *Aquitaine* to maybe send over a small task group to threaten that *Salonnian* base. It was just cheaper in the long run to pay spies to blow it up.

Rob wasn't surprised when the led him to a private tram car and pushed him in. He kept himself composed and relaxed. Hopefully, asking politely meant that someone just wanted to have a chat, rather than planning to make him disappear.

Rob kept himself smiling by reminding himself that Nigel and Roxy might just burn this whole damned planet down if something happened to him, officially or not.

Jorge would piss on the smoldering rubble.

Delightfully, the tram stopped at city hall and they walked him into the police station. Always a risk he would have never been seen again. Booking was perfunctory, consisting of them emptying his pockets for him and then chaining him to a table in an interrogation room.

Small time stuff. Rob had been through worse.

They left him to stew for a while, but Rob assumed he was under surveillance. He could count at least five cameras in here. Stone walls only roughly shaped. Table and three chairs, with him chained to the table. Enough light to make it almost office-like.

"Any chance someone could take me to the men's room?" Rob asked the room. "Gonna kinda be important soon."

No too soon, but might as well play dumb and helpful as long as he could.

Jorge had expected something official at some point. Now Rob just had to survive it. Whatever it was.

Maybe twenty minutes passed before the door opened. Right at the over/under for how long you let a suspect wait before you start talking to him. Long enough for the man to start to sweat, but not so long that he gets too angry to come around to cooperation.

Steafan Sìoltach, First Officer. Well dressed and calm. Alone, but again, at least five cameras watching, plus however many extra microphones and scanners in the suite.

Rob's hands were still cuffed, but in front of him now, resting on the table at the end of a three foot chain that would let him drink from a cup if they'd given him one.

Sìoltach had a mug of coffee in his hands that he placed on the far corner of the bolted-down table, out of reach. He also had a file folder about an inch thick with papers and probably other incriminating details.

Who knew what was illegal enough on *6940 Draconis* that the authorities would actually do something about it? I mean, technically, the laws here weren't that different than *Ramsey*, back home. But the enforcement left questions and ambiguities.

The new interrogator took the other chair and they stared at each other for a few minutes. Rob smiled more than the First Officer did, but that was just the play here. They wanted something, information most likely, rather than just shooting him in the back of the head.

"So is this on Finn's orders?" Rob asked simply, breaking the silence.

Sìoltach grimaced, aware that he might have already lost control of the interrogation, just from Rob's friendly tones, but not ceding an inch.

"Does it matter?" the man finally replied.

"Yes," Rob kept smiling. "Because if it does, the three of us should have a conversation without all the witnesses that will leak information you might want controlled in the future."

"I see," the man didn't, but it was a nice phrase to fill in the blanks.

But it also let Rob know that things were maybe bigger, deeper, and uglier than he had expected. Whatever he had expected.

"And bringing Finn down here to talk won't help?" the man asked.

"You trust your information security with everyone on the other end of all those cameras?" Rob asked. "Nobody going to pick up a comm and walk outside to make a quick call five minutes afterwards?"

That one hit home, but Rob had expected it to. Most government offices leaked like sieves on the best days. Bureaucrats were never paid enough in their own minds, and rich folks found it a cheap investment to provide a little side income for information. Occasionally, you even had ideologues with axes to grind.

Rob doubted the latter here, but someone would have put spies in place, or recruited some. Hell, he would have.

"And you think it would be worth the time and effort?" Sìoltach asked.

"You had me politely arrested and brought in," Rob said. "That means you want to talk. Personally, I've been waiting for the call, but didn't want to jump the gun, if you folks didn't end up being smart enough to put the pieces together."

Always the smile. Play the tough guy, but professional and understanding. Nothing prevented Sìoltach from just shooting him right now and leaving his body in a dumpster, except that new itch that maybe there was something more going on here.

Something that might upset all those careful calculations someone did yesterday when they issued a warrant for someone named Roberto Segura.

Handsome Rob leaned back and waited. Processing would be like the stages of death. It always was with people in this situation.

Faster than Rob expected, the man pulled out a comm from the inner pocket of his jacket and pushed a button.

"You home?" Sìoltach asked when the other end answered. "Bringing someone to see you. Wants to chat."

Sìoltach hung up and fixed Rob with heavy eyes. Not angry, but hard and unforgiving.

Always the smile.

"Someone get me the keys and a fresh set of cuffs," Sìoltach announced to the room.

Rob leaned forward conspiratorially.

"You'll also need my wallet," he whispered carefully. "You won't find what you need, but it's in there."

"Uh huh," Sìoltach replied.

A few minutes passed and the door opened. Three of the four goons from before, with shock wands and terrible smiles entered.

Rob stood as directed. Remained perfectly still as they unhooked him and then cuffed his hands in back again. Sìoltach had left, but now returned, eyes promising pain if this was all some terrible ruse.

Rudely, the man was holding Rob's own pulse pistol in one hand. Hopefully someone had determined that it worked just fine. Terrible to have them think the weapon was a fake and shoot him on a lark.

Sìoltach argued briefly with the cops, including the fourth one who had been out in the hall, in case Rob bolted for the door, but won and ordered them back to barracks. Or whatever cops did when they weren't beating up suspects. Probably a donut shop nearby.

"I will shoot you, if you give me any reason at all," Sìoltach promised as he grabbed hold of the cuffs.

"You want answers, First Officer," Rob looked back. "I'll provide some, but not in the public square. Simple as that."

Rather than heading out to the tram station again,

Sìoltach led him into a side corridor and into a section of the station Rob had never visited before. He had a rough idea where he was, and could backtrack perfectly to the police station, but would have had to pass through five secured portals to get there and didn't have the right tools.

Nigel and Roxy would have been able to get here pretty quickly, but they were like that.

He and Sìoltach ended up at a door in what looked like an upscale housing block.

"Stand here," Sìoltach stood Rob in front of a door and rang the bell.

The door opened a moment later and Rob was facing Finn Fukui and a bolter pistol.

"This better be good, Segura," the man growled as he stepped back.

Sìoltach gave Rob enough push to get him going.

"You have no idea, Governor," Rob promised.

20

———

Finn kept the punk across the room as Steafan moved him in and sat the guy down on a chair pulled in from the dining area and turned around backwards. They left his hands cuffed.

The room was secured and had been swept this morning. The door was locked and Steafan had dropped all the locks into place.

"Who are you working for?" Finn demanded, still holding the bolter in the punk's general direction.

"*Lincolnshire*'s Guardia Civil Interior," Segura surprised him by replying immediately. "The *Service*."

"And I'm supposed to believe that?" Finn asked sarcastically.

"I'm running an operation that is not targeting you or *6940 Draconis* in any way, Governor," the stranger replied calmly. "I can prove it, if you're willing to talk."

"Can you now?" Finn let the doubt paint the whole room. "How?"

Segura turned to Steafan now.

"You grabbed my wallet, right?" he asked.

"I did," Steafan replied. "But there's nothing in there. We scanned it."

"Your scanners are junior varsity, First Officer," Segura said with a hint of disdain. "Useful against amateurs, but not professional grade. If you're nice to me sometime, maybe over some whiskey, I'll tell you how to upgrade them."

That probably stung more than a woman's slap, from the flinch. Steafan took his job seriously. Finn knew that. Suggesting that waltzing past it was child's play was a low blow, but it would also guarantee that they both were listening, which was obviously Segura's intent.

Steafan pulled out the wallet from an inside jacket pocket now. Brown leather. Not too badly aged, but not brand new either. Four inches wide by maybe twice that tall, capable of holding bills without folding them in half.

"Inside, you'll find a picture of Mrs. Jones," Segura said calmly. "A cheesecake photo showing her topless and with all the naughty bits artfully shadowed. It was tucked in at the back, but I presume you pulled everything out and cataloged it, so I have no idea where it is now."

Steafan emptied the whole thing onto the coffee table. Cash, business cards, local photo ID, the other, random things a man accumulates in his wallet over time.

The picture of Mrs. Jones was there. Fantastic, as it showed her kneeling on a bed in a bedroom, turned slightly, playful and smiling at the camera. There were no tan lines at all.

"This one?" Steafan asked sarcastically.

"Yes," Segura said. "Go into the kitchen and run it under warm water for a few minutes."

"What do you expect will happen?" Finn asked.

Segura smiled at him now. A real smile.

"The Service printed that picture over the top of my Identity card," he said. "It won't scan with anything short of a full X-ray machine, and nobody in his right mind would damage that card if they stole it or found it lost on the sidewalk. That's a collector's item."

"I see," Finn replied. "How did you get it?"

"The woman only appears to be demure and matronly, Governor," Segura said. "In her youth, back in the drugs and booze days, she did all sorts of crazy shit. The Service got hold of that photo and used it to disguise my papers. Other agents have other tricks, but since I was traveling with Mrs. Jones, they decided that it would be the perfect cover."

Finn nodded to Steafan, watched his second best friend disappear into the kitchen. The sound of running water, the air systems, and his heartbeat were the other things Finn heard for several minutes.

Finally, Steafan returned, a look of awe on his face like Finn had never seen before.

"Shit," was all he said as he handed Finn a piece of hard plastic.

The face was the same. Roberto Segura. Six-Foot-One. One-Ninety-Five. Black eyes. Black Hair. Hispanic genotype. Field Agent, Guardia Civil Interior.

The man was a damned spy. Right here in his living room. Finn was tempted to shoot him, but getting blood out of the carpet was nearly impossible, and Aoki would never forgive him for ruining their living room.

"Why are you here?" Finn growled, deep and angry.

Segura fixed him with those hard eyes and lost all the laughter and comradery that had been there two seconds ago.

"A *Salonnian* Syndicate has built a semi-secret operational base on the surface of *6725 Lacertae*," he replied calmly. "Not all that far from the borders with both *Corynthe* and *Lincolnshire*, especially since *6940 Draconis* sticks out like a thumb."

"And?" Finn prompted.

Segura took a breath and glanced at Steafan before he continued.

"My orders are to see it destroyed, without involving the *Lincolnshire* navy, or getting *Aquitaine* to do anything about it," Segura finally admitted. "To do so, the Service invented the cover of funding a movie. Royo and Jones are out of work and desperate, so they won't ask too many questions, as long as the catering holds out. Same with Framingham, although your wife has made my mission much more complex by actually finding Longbow artists he likes."

"That's not a cover?" Finn asked.

He had been getting regular reports, third-hand, from both Aoki and one of the musicians involved.

"No," Segura almost sounded disgusted. "Longbow's suddenly serious about recording a second album, after happily working for Royo doing soundtracks and such for over a decade. So now I have to juggle that as well, because the man mentioned a tour, day before yesterday."

"So why are you here on Draconic?" Steafan stepped around in front of Segura.

"My hope was that we could recruit one or more local motherships," Segura said. "As well as a team of armed combat experts, which is where I presume you panicked. The plan was to literally film the entire assault on *6725 Lacertae* and include that as stock footage. Same with whatever mothership and crews we could bring in. Royo's a damned perfectionist, wanting honest to goodness pirates, rather than actors who play them. Under cover of getting him real pirates to pal around with, I was going to go blow up a *Salonnian* base and let the pirates loot it's bones clean, like ants."

"That's completely insane, Segura," Finn choked the words out.

"Yes. Yes it is," the man admitted with a smile. "And so audacious that nobody would ever believe the truth. Rumors and miscommunications would make it look like the pirates took advantage of our filming schedule to go score a raid they could deny later, telling everyone it was just a movie. Royo and Jones would go along, because I'm providing the funding to make what would turn out to be an amazingly-realistic film, and they're nothing but actors."

"You want to get us into a shooting incident with *Salonnia*?" Finn forced himself to be calm.

On the face of it, the man was right. The audacity was so over the top that he could probably pull it off.

"Not *Salonnia*," Segura corrected him. "One of the Syndicates, *Ahearn & Toledanoi*. Plus, you people are pirates, and known to be at odds with your own government, so you aren't about to listen to orders from Jessica or David to behave if there is money to be made. Finally, you aren't involved, Governor. This is me and a couple of the local captains engaging in a private business transaction that just happens to mess with one of your competitors while protecting your position. You aren't trading with that secret naval base in *Salonnian* space."

Finn marveled at the enormity of it. The spies had apparently written the script with Royo and Jones in mind, knowing they could swindle a couple of broke actors into doing it. *Ahearn & Toledanoi* didn't trade with *6940 Draconis*, so while there had been rumors of a new base, they had been muddled up in the general intelligence summaries of problems on the other side of the border.

"So say I were to believe you, Segura," Finn began, having processed things about as well as he could at present. "And didn't just throw your ass into a cell or exile you to the surface. Then what?"

"Then I tell everyone I had to pay off hell of a fine," Segura said. "Please don't make it too big, because I've only got so much budget to work with here, but this situation was not unanticipated. Your people continue to watch me like hawks, as they have been. At some point, Royo or Jones use their charms to bring in a fish big enough, and we go off for some filming. Once off-world, we convince them to really attack someone, playing to their chaotic and juvenile delinquency tendencies and their greed. You have plausible deniability as does *Lincolnshire*."

"And you've been talking to Nakano," Steafan said.

"Loosely," Segura admitted. "We can't get a straight answer out of him who we works for. I'd hate to hire him to raid his own damned base. Man like Nakano might go for it, with enough money on the table, but he might also blow the entire operation. Too risky to nail down details until we have that one."

"Kozel wouldn't talk?" Steafan grinned. "Not that impressed, once she got you into bed?"

"Neither of us was able to even walk straight when we were done. First Officer," Segura smiled. "Let alone plan a palace revolution. And believe me, I probed her for every opening that presented itself."

"Last I checked, Okonkwo Nakano was working for *Black Aurora*," Finn decided to play along. "At least that's what my spies have told me. Going after Bergier targets and shipping, as well as the usual piratical things around here, like slipping deeper into *Corynthe* space or crossing over to *Lincolnshire*. Does that open the way for you to get deeper into trouble?"

"It does, Governor," Segura said. "Why the change of heart?"

"You'll owe me one, son," Finn smiled cruelly at the man. "Or your Service will. And Nakano is a *Salonnian* spy, so there's a damned good chance his masters get pissed at him for freelancing. Plus he might suffer serious damage raiding a *Ahearn & Toledanoi* base, and end up being less of a threat around here. Be a shame if he had to face a restless crew for a few years."

"You are a cold, hard man, Governor," Segura said with apparent respect in his eyes. "And yes, I will let my superiors know we owe you one when I get back. How they'll deal with it is beyond my control, but my government considers *Corynthe* to be less of a threat these days, because of Queen Jessica, and have concentrated their efforts on *Salonnia*. If you want to help, I'm sure they'd be happy to negotiate some funding to cause the Syndicates more grief."

"What about *Fribourg*?" Finn asked, calling up a stellar map in his head. "*Salonnia* is a client of the *Empire*, and there is peace between all the major players right now."

"There is a lack of active shooting at each other, Governor," Segura corrected him. "*Salonnia* is still run by crime families. *Corynthe* has a Pirate Queen. The *Empire* is a fragile place as the man in charge apparently wants to start a war with somebody deep in the galactic interior. We have to protect ourselves from predators."

"You are a predator, Segura," Finn said.

"As are you, Governor," the spy replied.

Finn considered the situation.

"I can't just return your ID to you with your wallet," Finn said. "Everything will be cataloged before they release you."

"Like I can argue with them that you stole a topless picture of Mrs. Jones?" Segura laughed. "They'll just be mad you did it before they got a chance to make a copy."

Finn laughed. The man had a point. She was among the most beautiful women in the galaxy, and he could see the rumors.

Aoki would need to know the truth, but that was a given anyway. Especially if Longbow was in a position to mess up

Segura's chance to hammer one of the Syndicates hard enough that they fell over.

"Okay, Segura," Finn stood and clicked the safety on his bolter. "I'm willing to give you a chance. And yes, the next screw up is probably terminal, so behave accordingly. Steafan, take him back and let him rot in a cell overnight. Figure out a good enough fine to make me happy and get cash out of the man before you release him."

Steafan took charge of the prisoner and departed as Finn studied the card in his hand.

Roberto Segura. *Lincolnshire* spy posing as a film producer. About to attempt one of the most audacious cons Finn had ever heard of, with a larger than life cast.

Finn wondered if the man might consider working some freelance gigs on the side.

21

EVERYONE WAS IN THE SUITE WHEN ROB OPENED THE door and walked in. In retrospect, he shouldn't have been surprised, but Nigel had gone so far as to bring in one of Longbow's amplifier cases that happened to be filled with small arms, if you opened the secret compartments just right.

"Status?" Jorge asked, only after Rob had closed and locked the door behind him.

"I'm blown, but the rest of the operation may or may not have the semi-official blessing of the Governor," Rob replied, filling a mug of coffee and taking a spot at the table.

Longbow had his medkit handy, next to a holstered pistol hanging from the back of his chair. Roxy had six ammunition magazines for a bolter rifle lined up on the table in front of her, with the weapon itself holding the seventh and leaned next to her. Nigel was tweaking that camera of his. The one that supposedly fired missiles. Jorge had settled for a shoulder holster and a pulse pistol identical to the one Rob had gotten returned. The only person missing was Raef, but that meant she was probably getting the ship ready to run like hell in the middle of a firefight.

Everyone relaxed some as he sat.

"Talk to me, kid," Jorge ordered.

Rob quickly filled them in, with Jorge adding details around the comm call he had gotten from a waitress.

"So I paid the fine this morning, got all my stuff back, and one of the cops handed me a tram coin to get me home," Rob said. "I need a shower, a shave, and breakfast. In that order."

"Kid, you got off cheap," Jorge laughed. "Last time that happened to me, I ended owing about double that."

"You hadn't had your cover blown," Rob guessed. "I asked him to keep it cheap because that was coming out of my operations budget, and I got the impression that keeping us in the field damages his enemies in all sort of delightful and probably unexpected ways. In short, we're playing the stalking horse for whatever other gigs the governor thinks will come up."

"So we stand down?" Longbow asked, looking back and forth between he and Jorge.

"Far as I'm concerned, nothing official changes," Rob said.

"And the Governor confirms *Black Aurora*?" Jorge asked Rob. "This is where either we blow things open or it all slots into place neatly."

"That's what he's willing to own up to," Rob corrected the assumption. "Maybe he's setting us up, maybe not."

"I'm willing to chance it," Jorge decided. "You meet your girlfriend on the dock when her shuttle comes in and see if she can be seduced. Play it as tight as you need, but assume I'll be arranging a meeting with Nakano to bring him aboard. *Queen of the Borders* is already pretty much signed and delivered at this point as our troop transport, although he thinks most of them are filming crew and extras, rather than combat troops. But the money was good enough and so was the part where he gets to play the villain, when we go back and film all the dramatic roles later.

"He's not setting up a double-cross?" Roxy asked.

"Oh, I'm sure they all are," Jorge laughed. "But they think a double will be enough on this one. I've got so many pieces in motion that they'll all be confused. Same with Handsome. By the time it all gets out, everyone will assume they were part of the biggest practical joke ever played. And there's something to be said for that, but not the way they'll expect. Now, Longbow, what trouble have you caused?"

Rob watched the man shrug and relax, falling out of himself and back into who he normally played. Gone, the combat medic. Back the melancholy rocker.

"We have a rough cut of an album," he said. "Twelve songs recorded well enough that a little studio magic could probably make them releasable. Not sure what the hell to do with it, since there was a chance we were going to be in a firefight this morning and I'd have to abandon everyone. Again."

"Last time wasn't my fault, Levi," Jorge said sternly. "I warned you she was trouble on day one. You chose to ignore my gut instinct."

"True, but still," Longbow sighed. "For the first time, in more than twenty years, it might be possible. I mean really possible to finish this thing. And do it right."

Rob watched Jorge's eyes narrow. You could almost hear the gears engage and grind as Jorge calculated odds and angles.

"What would happen if we decided to take this show on the road?" Jorge asked suddenly. "Instead of necessarily filming a movie on them, we change skins in space, after we've left. Round up your friends and have a tour? Maybe we hire all those goons as tour security for a cover. You've got a new album and we pull a variant of the old broken-down tour bus when *Queen of the Borders* suddenly drops into orbit and has a nav malfunction."

"At a minimum, that puts us in a studio for a week with Alicia under a deadline," Longbow said, smiling just the littlest bit. "She prefers that sort of thing, says it focuses her. We might land planetside with hardened chips to sell or give away, so we'll need a couple of pallets of blanks to burn. Nigel?"

"Will add it to the list," the cowboy nodded seriously. "Lined up a supplier, just in case. He'll need three days for one pallet. I'll need to see about getting a second."

Somehow, Rob wasn't surprised that Nigel was that far ahead of everyone with his planning. His job was the hardest, since he had to play defense constantly, while outguessing Jorge's crazy stunts so he had access to whatever gear the team might need.

Like Jorge suddenly becoming a band manager and Rob handling bookings. He knew Roxy could sing. The woman could do almost anything if she set her mind to it. And the extra cachet of impersonating the real Mrs. Jones would be hilarious, although they might actually list Roxy under her real name and tell everyone it was a cover.

"You're already deep into it, aren't you, kid?" Jorge was scowling this way.

"Mrs. Jones should join the other females singing backup on the final recording," Rob said simply. "Then we're back to before, with Nigel handling sound, me running interference, and you impressing the hell out of everyone."

"It's hell, being me," Jorge announced, taking a sip of martini.

Rob laughed. Fukui's seduction of Longbow might just blow up in everyone's faces so spectacularly that nobody knew what hit them. And it might put them into the right spot at the right time.

22

———————

The settlement had mellowed out some in the week since Rob had gotten into and out of jail, but there was an element of wildness tonight that hadn't been there yesterday. Almost a musk in the air or something.

He had nailed down a platoon of armed men whose scores and backgrounds he liked. Veterans who would only bitch the usual amount when they found out that everything had changed yet again. Especially since they were still getting paid for training and might not even have to shoot anyone, if everything went well.

And he had left a message for Lilijana when she got back to the surface from wherever *Wild Duck* had gone in the last two weeks. That wasn't enough time to really raid someone, unless you had perfect intelligence on the target going in.

It was, however, enough time to bluff your way in the front door and surprise someone with a loaded gun they hadn't been expecting, like Rob or Jorge had done more than once.

No, what concerned him was that they had been gone just long enough to run someplace like *6725 Lacertae* and

137

back, spending a day picking up and dropping off supplies and getting more information from the folks on the ground. Or warning them.

But that was just paranoia speaking. It was also enough time to go lots of other places. Nakano just played his cards too close to the vest for anyone to really know what the man was doing, and his crew didn't talk.

Rob practically smelled her as he entered the bar. Might not have recognized her, though, except he was paying attention and hoping she would come.

Lilijana wasn't dressed like a pirate officer tonight. Gone were the long boots and leggings and shirt and jacket. Instead, she wore a royal blue dress like a sheath for a sword over her glowing skin, with a gold sash tied around the middle to emphasize her muscles and curves even more than being sleeveless. Her strawberry blond hair was almost long enough to grab a handful in a sweaty moment, but not quite.

Rob let his eyes get big and appreciative as she walked right up to the table and lurked over him.

"Wow," Rob said by way of introduction.

"I had considered just blowing you off," she replied. "Leave you dangling, lest you get the idea that I might be your beck and call girl."

"I'm happy you changed your mind," Rob gestured for her to join him in the booth.

"Nope," she shook her head with a smile. "You're taking me dancing."

Rob nodded and slid towards her. She didn't step back when he stood up, so it was almost like climbing a girlie tree as Rob got to his feet. There might have been a little too much rubbing and touching as he did.

"Whatever I can do to please you, madam," Rob held out the crook of his arm for her to take as they finally got untangled.

Not exactly the way he had intended to probe the woman for socio-politically perilous answers, but there were worse ways to go about it, especially if she wanted to step outside herself for an evening and be treated like a woman, instead of having to be the toughest man on the crew to get any respect.

"We'll talk about that, too," she smiled enigmatically up at him.

Outside, they headed to the nearest tram station. She skipped the first train as being too crowded and picked the second. They ended up in a car by themselves, so he turned and extracted himself enough to look at her.

"Jorge's also got a message out for your Captain," Rob began.

"I know," she nodded. "Okonkwo told me, so I presumed that it would be good news and we should celebrate."

"Just so," Rob smiled. "I'll hope you are as good at keeping this secret as the others. Jorge would like to hire you, Nakano, and *Wild Duck*. But he wants to do something over and above that, and those two will be negotiating fees and such."

"Oh?" her eyes got big. They were blue glaciers. "And what would law-abiding citizens like you need with pirates like us?"

"Jorge wants the most realistic footage he can get," Rob said carefully. "So we've hired some experts in ground combat to assault a lunar base belonging to some folks nobody around here particularly likes."

Let her do the math. Two plus two, but still.

"And *Wild Duck*?" her voice turned a little breathless.

"Your job would be to drop the hammer on the base, once those folks have disabled it," Rob continued. "We'll film everything, and *Wild Duck* gets whatever salvage it can haul away from the wreckage. Afterwards, we'll come back here to build soundstages and shoot the rest of the movie."

"That's crazy," she said.

"Jorge demands verisimilitude," he replied. "And he has the funding, if *Wild Duck* can be hired cheap enough to clean up after the troops break in and do the deed. The studio work is actually pretty cheap, since we don't have to pay union scale around here for talent, having recruited certain persons we would like to put in front of the camera."

"So where is this place that's about to get a dose of pirates?" she asked, her eyes growing darker and almost heavier, if he had to pick a word.

"It's a secret for now," he leaned down and kissed her lightly to take the sting out of the words. "Jorge won't even tell Nakano until we've got everything nailed down with contracts, but they are going over plans in the near future. If your boss is in, hopefully you'll be in as well?"

"Wouldn't miss it," she kissed him with more verve, but they had to stop as the tram arrived at their destination.

Outside, they went into the main part of the nearest building, following the thumping of the music, rumbling through the ground at them.

The club was insanely packed. Rob, however, had already made it a point to bribe all the bouncers up front better than normal previously, so he got escorted past the rope line and into the joint like royalty.

Seriously, just hanging out with Jorge was teaching him all sorts of things he needed, in order to be a movie star. Briefly, Rob wondered if he should add some formal acting classes to the training the Service gave him, so he could put himself into a few movie roles, perhaps with Jorge.

What would it be like to be *That Guy*? The face everybody recognized but without the name attached. Creator knew he was probably going to start being recognizable at some point. Might as well be able to twist it sideways as a deflection.

At the bar, his favorite babe was tending in the middle. Underdressed and overstuffed into a top that just barely kept her contained. Interesting ink in her skin flowed off under her clothing in ways that made you want to tear off all her clothes, just so you could read her.

It made an interesting story, when you did.

She grinned at him and handed over a pair of glasses in trade for a bill and a smile. She was always working nights, so breakfast or an early dinner was the best way to hang out.

Rob handed one glass to Lilijana and sipped his own, threading his way to the back of the club, where another pair of bouncers isolated a section of the club for big shots. Rob didn't have a reservation, but he had friends with these folks, so they found him a spot quickly enough.

Mostly, it was a place to keep the glasses from being stolen or tampered with while he and this lovely lady danced.

And they danced.

Rob came back with tall glasses of water at one point, just because he was sweating at least as much as she was. Probably more exhausted, but she had been going like the world was going to end in a few hours, so he wasn't about to dissuade her.

Sometime after midnight, she looked up and him with a fire in those bright, blue eyes.

"Okay, I'm done," she said. "We're going back to my place now."

Rob had wondered if he would have to cry uncle first, but all the aerobics he'd been doing at least let him keep up. He rose and she took his hand as they made their way out the front and back to the subway station. It wasn't all that crowded, but it also wasn't empty. Being underground, the city tended to go pretty much all the time, just cycling up and down in waves, like a lazy tide.

A tram stopped and Lilijana guided him aboard, her hands roaming around under his jacket as they did. Her head was against his shoulder as well. It was most distracting.

But something caught his eye as they sat. Maybe the way those two men stood, clear at the back of the car, well away from him and the woman, but not the least bit relaxed. Guards on duty had that particular gleam in their eyes when they watched you approach.

There were four of them. Two together and two more separated and patently ignoring each other, but somehow watching him in ways he couldn't have explained, except to call it magic.

Field Agent training focused on knowing when you were being watched. Better to ignore a meet with a source rather than lead the authorities to a mole in their organization. And you had to be casual as you kept moving, leading them away from the scene of the not-quite crime so they wouldn't know where to look, if they did see someone they knew.

Could be a coffee shop. Maybe on a park bench. Or brushing up against someone on a tram like this one.

Those men set off every one of his personal alarms. It wasn't like the four cops that had come to arrest him. Those men hadn't been aiming for subtle. These men were, but something about they gave off the wrong smell.

Rob didn't panic, but he didn't want to alarm Lilijana, especially if she hadn't noticed. He could always grab her and bounce off a tram at a stop, drawing his pistol fast enough if trouble came with him.

He turned to nuzzle her hair and kiss her ear. It let him look backwards at the pair at the same time he slid a hand into a pocket and triggered the little alarm function on his comm. Nigel had programmed it, cracking the case itself open so he could solder in the extra bits in such a way that the little computer inside the comm didn't know about them.

Somewhere, Nigel would come up out of a dead sleep, if he was. Hopefully, the cavalry would find him and it would all be a terrible misunderstanding. He could call and give Jorge and password that indicated he was fine.

But everything was wrong, all of a sudden.

"How close to your stop?" Rob murmured seductively in her ear.

"Two stops," she replied as she kissed him. "Why?"

"Don't like the looks of the folks riding with us," Rob said. "Prepare to bolt off the tram when the doors open. I want some space if they mean trouble."

She glanced back and snuggled a little tighter.

"Actually, it's entirely different," Lilijana said in a harsh voice. "They're with me and we'd like to ask you some questions, Segura."

Oh, shit.

Suddenly, there was a pistol stuffed into his stomach. Not his, but there was no way he could even move without her pulling the trigger.

Rob decided to play stupid anyway.

"What's going on, babe?" he asked, tilting his head away from her far enough to look at her face.

It was no longer a face he recognized. The bones were the same. As was the skin. However, there was a different person inhabiting them. An angry one.

"You're a spy," she said. "We don't like spies."

Honestly, what happened to the woman he had just spent three hours dancing and necking with?

A hand suddenly descended on his neck, grabbing hard and holding him in place in his seat.

Lilijana's other hand snaked inside his coat and pulled the

pulse pistol out, handing it to someone behind Rob that he couldn't see.

"Don't do anything to make me shoot you, Segura," she snarled at him.

He noted that there wasn't the promise that maybe this was all a misunderstanding that could be cleared up later. No, this was the disappear down a rabbit hole scenario.

Thank the Creator he had managed to trigger the panic button. Assuming the gang could get here before something irretrievable happened.

They passed one tram stop, and Rob watched the five people around him in the glass of the car. Movement was curtailed by the hand on his neck, and the man guarding the door against anyone wanting to ride this tram.

The doors closed like a guillotine blade falling.

Into the darkness of another tunnel.

"This is our stop coming up, Handsome," she said bluntly. "You will stand slowly and walk with care onto the platform, where we will guide you to the suite where a conversation will occur. Or I'll just shoot you right here."

She didn't mean that, did she?

Still, Rob noted the shock wands in two hands. And the guns. Whatever close combat training he had mastered to be a Field Agent wasn't going to mean a whole bunch against this group. The best he could do was walk casually and stall while a silent ping for help went out into the aether.

Movement ended and the doors opened. One man went out immediately and Rob rose with care. Shock wands suck. He was surrounded by the four men on the platform as locals exited other cars, so everyone stood still and waited for the platform to clear.

Lilijana took point, her snub bolter held low against her thigh like a professional. Another man followed her. Three followed him.

"This way," she opened a panel that looked like a maintenance hallway.

Inside, they were alone. The floor was just dusty enough that Rob could note tracks down the middle and taste staleness in the air. Lights were every twenty yards, leaving pools of darkness you emerged from like a skipped rock kissing the surface of a still lake.

There was nowhere to run now, other than straight back to where he had been, but that just put him on the tram platform with five angry, armed people chasing him.

A hand shoved his shoulder, nearly knocking him down. Rob considered tripping and falling, just to slow things up, but suspected that he'd get a few kicks to the head and ribs if he did.

Better to remain conscious and mobile.

After a long walk, the woman turned to a side hallway and took the group into the maintenance spaces of one of the tower blocks. Past elevator shafts and HVAC installations that always reminded Rob of grungy modern art.

The space here looked like the back of one of Jorge's sets. Pretty for the camera, but raw and industrial on this side. Lighting was rather random. Just enough to see by, but not read.

Lilijana opened a heavy, metal door and led them down a flight of steps. Again, Rob walked carefully, but not slow enough to provoke anyone with a fist or weapon handy. This was an access space for workers, rather than tenants.

Two stories down, she exited into a better-maintained corridor. People lived here, although none were in evidence at the moment. Still, narrow spaces and out-numbered.

Rob continued to stall for time.

The apartment had a number on it, as they directed him in. There was a single, wooden chair in the middle of what would have been the living room, with the other furniture pulled well back. The floor was concrete in here, so if they killed him in the process, the blood would be easy enough to clean up later.

"Sit," the woman ordered in an ugly voice.

Rob got shoved into place, but didn't resist too much. They'd just shock wand him at this point. That shit hurt.

Someone took his jacket off and then tied his hands behind him. It was rope, rather than metal cuffs, for all the good that did him. Wasn't like he was wearing his combat tuxedo, where the cufflinks came with a small cutting laser built in for exactly this sort of situation.

Rob made a note to dress better on his next seduction, just for the extra toys Nigel had added to what the Service considered standard gear.

All his pockets got emptied onto a metal, dining room table nearby: wallet, comm, cash, pulse pistol, pocket change, accumulated business cards. The mark of the modern hustler.

Fortunately, nobody joined the group. Rob's only real fear at this point was someone with a black bag filled with chemicals. He could be blown, but if they put him under sedation and started digging into his back story, he would also blow Jorge and the rest.

They probably just would shoot him at that point. Especially when he told them that he'd called for help.

One man guarding the apartment door. Another standing in the kitchen out of the way and watching over the counter. The two with shock wands here in the living room, flanking Lilijana, still holding her snub loosely in one hand.

In a mark of bizarre irony, Rob didn't even have his ID card anywhere handy. It had gotten returned by courier in a plain envelope, and Jorge had promptly destroyed it. The Governor knew who he was now, and nobody else would benefit from that knowledge. It would give Rob one more get out of jail free moment, but he doubted that something like that would save him at this point.

"So who do you really work for?" Rob asked.

These people didn't look like trained pros. There were subtle indicators about the stance and face if you knew what to look for. Deadly amateurs, probably, which was worse. Amateurs made mistakes that frequently, accidentally turned terminal.

Although this situation already looked terminal, at least far as Lilijana's eyes seemed to promise him.

"I'll ask the questions, Segura," she growled.

That answered that. He had wondered if he had pissed off the Governor again, but she would have said that, rather than get angry.

Deadly amateurs.

"Are you from *Petron*?" she demanded.

Behind her, one of the men tapped his hand with the shaft of a shock wand. Probably meant to frighten folks.

Rob made a note to feed the stick to the man when he got loose, as a dessert that followed every single tooth in his mouth, which would get kicked in first.

"*Petron*?" Rob let himself go confused. "The capital world?"

"That's right," Lilijana said. "We know you're a spy. We have someone in the Governor's office who told us."

I doubt that, lady. If they knew, you wouldn't have to ask me.

"I have never been to *Petron* in my life, Kozel," Rob replied steadily. It was even the truth.

"Then who are you working for?" she countered.

"Not sure what you're talking about," Rob said. "What's all this about?"

It was a provocation. They trained you how to do that sort of thing while being interrogated.

Rob had expected an open palm slap. You could put a lot of torque and sting into that sort of strike, while not damaging your target appreciably. Instead, she punched him. Slugged him right in the jaw with the fist not holding the gun, thank the gods.

Rob hadn't see that coming, so it shocked him that she was going for violence already. He found himself laying painfully on his hands when she overbalanced the chair backwards.

The spare goon stepped up and bodily lifted Rob and his chair back to vertical as Rob flexed the muscles in his face. Might as well play like you've just gotten your bell rung.

Rob blinked and shook his head a few times before focusing most of his attention on the woman in the middle of his trouble. But then, women had frequently been the center of Rob's troubles. This woman seemed more likely to kill him that most of them had been.

He needed to string thing out. Not get himself killed before help could arrive. They needed something, or she probably would have just shot him already.

"Feel like talking?" she sneered.

Concussions do interesting things to your head. The Service intentionally put their agents through the trauma, just so they knew how to react. It was a chemical they could inject that gave you the same symptoms. And made you puke your guts empty about five hours later.

Rob had hated the smell of that vial they used. It still made him homicidal, just to think about it, years later.

"What?" Rob yelled, like he had gone half-deaf from the blow. He twisted his head right and left a little, just for emphasis.

"Can you hear me?" she raised her voice louder now and stepped close enough that he could kick her, if he felt like feeling the loving caress of the shock wand in the hands of a thug.

"Sort of," he yelled back.

Her hearing was fine, so he could rattle her even more with the volume. The walls were stone or metal, so it wasn't like they would wake the neighbors.

"Who are you working for?" she demanded again."

"Jorge," Rob replied, sticking for now to his cover.

Plus, like *Petron*, it was technically the truth. And technical was the best kind of truth.

She kicked him this time. Deliberately cracked him with the toe of her shoe.

"Maybe next time I'll break your kneecap," she promised. "They snap, you know, particularly well you get under them just right with the pointed toe of a woman's pump like this."

She held it up for him to examine

Rob wasn't faking the pain this time.

"Answer me," she snarled, coming right down into his face.

It was still a pretty snarl, even on the face of a psychopath. Rob took a deep breath and leaned back, pretending to be overawed by the threat of violence in her stance. Punching him in the balls wouldn't require much effort on her part right now. Probably was next on her list.

"I can't tell you," Rob let his voice fall much quieter.

"Oh, Handsome, I don't think you understand the situation," she purred, caressing the impending bruise on his face with something like velvet delicacy. "If you don't tell me, I'm going to have these men hurt you. Badly. That would be a bad thing."

She surprised the hardened Field Agent by kissing him on the forehead lightly before she stepped back and studied him from the middle distance. It was almost as though she hadn't been playing a role before the psychotic killer had shown up.

Maybe *Wild Duck* had gone somewhere and she had gotten new orders? If Nakano tried this stunt with Jorge and Roxy, *Wild Duck* would be needing a new captain. And replacements for however many crew members had walked into that meeting. Not that it would help him right now, but if his friends had to burn that damned ship to the ground, that would be okay.

Not like Rob was going to forgive and forget on this one.

Rob did the math in his head. It had been about fifteen minutes since he triggered the alarm. No idea how long to round up Longbow, but Roxy was probably in the suite and Jorge was actually more deadly with a pistol dead drunk than he was sober. Something to do with the amount of experience both ways, Rob guessed.

"What's it going to be, Handsome?" she said, loud, but not yelling.

"They'll kill me," Rob cringed.

"If you don't talk, I'll kill won't just kill you, but we'll take the time to maim you first. And enjoy doing it," she said, sounding as hot and bothered as she had when they'd been snuggled close together the other night.

Good to know. You could have said something like *We'll protect you* instead. I might not have believed you, but *in vino veritas*, lady.

Same in rage.

However, it also clarified Rob's thought processes. Now he just had to string this conversation out long enough.

"*Lincolnshire*," Rob admitted in a quiet, defensive voice, hoping he wasn't about to get shot on general principles. Some people might panic at this point.

"Wait," Lilijana stomped closer again, anger giving way to confusion. "Did you say *Lincolnshire?*"

This was where the manipulation earlier started to bear fruit. She had lost control of the conversation again. Everyone forgot that the Service played offence, even as *Lincolnshire*'s navy was too small and weak to threaten their neighbors.

"That's right," Rob cringed more, folding in on himself as much as he could like he was expecting another blow.

"What's your target then?" she demanded.

Rob had forgotten the old maxim. Your enemy isn't nine feet tall. Just remember that they aren't three feet tall, either.

"What?" he tried weakly, right on the edge of panic.

"Who are you planning to attack?" Lilijana loomed over him now.

"*Salonnia.*" Rob figured he could let the details out slowly enough at this point.

Just waiting for the cavalry to come over the hill.

"And have *Corynthe* take the blame?" she mused, changing personalities again on him. "Interesting. That explains the interest in *Black Aurora* and *Ahearn & Toledano*. Stupid of you to hire Okonkwo to attack his own bosses, unless you had something on him, or could offer enough money to turn the man's head. Too bad you guessed wrong."

She paused now, studying him like a freshly-butchered hog.

It was about to get really ugly. Particularly when she put down the pistol and picked up the knife that had apparently been waiting for her on the mantle.

She dialed someone on her comm and waited for them to pick up as she studied the knife in her hands, watching the light shine across the blade.

"*6725 Lacertae*," she smiled at him as she spoke into the microphone. "Brilliant, Handsome, I'll give you that."

It wasn't a question, so he didn't bother to reply. Instead, he slumped his shoulders in apparent defeat.

Plus, to make himself a smaller target as she started to cut pieces off of him. It wouldn't be long now.

"Understood," she replied.

Now was then things got dicey. He was blown, but he'd known that. Would they bring him in someplace to slowly bleed him dry of whatever he knew, or shoot him right there and cut their losses? The Service had trained agents how to withstand torture, but that presumed the interrogator wanted information.

This chick just wanted blood.

Lilijana Kozel had a smile in her eyes still, but the woman was apparently either a trained agent in her own right, or a homicidal sociopath.

Rob would put his money in the latter, just from the look in her eyes.

"Now, Handsome…" she started to say, taking a step towards him with the shining knife out.

The door to the apartment exploded inward, carrying the man guarding it into the room on the shockwave.

Rob went over sideways onto his left as hard and fast as he could.

Roxy came through the door first, holding that bolter rifle up to her shoulder. Anybody but her, and he would have pitched a fit about not using a pistol in close quarters like this. But he'd seen her scores back home.

Jorge was a step behind her, amazingly without a martini glass in hand for once. Truly, a measure of the seriousness of the situation.

Roxy blew past the kitchen space where the one goon was without pausing, that bolter barking quickly twice, and then a third time.

Rob craned his head around fast enough to see the first goon blasted backwards into the wall. Lilijana got flipped ass over tea kettle from the shot hitting her.

The last man standing had started to move, and Rob kicked at him with a foot. Not much, but unexpected. The man faceplanted as Roxy sidestepped and drove him into the floor with the butt of her rifle and then put a shot into his back.

Elapsed time, less than three seconds.

Jorge rolled Rob over and cut the rope with a knife as Roxy disarmed Lilijana, kicking the knife away.

"Kitchen?" Rob asked.

"Mine," Jorge said. "Down."

Looking around the room, Rob was surprised the pirate lady was still alive, but Roxy had apparently shifted her aim high and left from center. The shoulder was probably shattered, but modern medicine could do wonders.

"Nigel was listening to comm traffic," Jorge said as he helped Rob to his feet. "We're blown."

"Maybe," Rob countered. "How close is *Queen* to ready?"

Jorge paused to study him.

"Hit them anyway?" he asked.

"Ticking bomb scenario," Rob replied. "But we've still got enough fuse to burn. Any message has to either jump on the first ship and blow their own cover, or go through channels. That buys us time."

"What do we do with her?" Roxy asked, standing over the only other pirate in the room still alive.

It was a nasty wound, but Roxy had intentionally kept her alive. Even an of inch down and over and it would be a sucking chest wound and impending death. This could be treated, if someone called the medics fast enough.

Longbow wasn't here, so they must have decided not to wait. Rob could agree with those decisions. It had been his ass on the line in another few seconds.

Rob retrieved all his kit as a chance to think. The others were deferring to him, since he'd been in the room.

"We've got it all on tape, Nigel?" he yelled to the front of the apartment, where the cowboy was covering the hallway and listening to the comms. "Plus what my comm was recording?"

"Do, Handsome," came the reply.

He turned to Lilijana.

Even through the pain he could see the snarl on her face.

"It's too late for you, Handsome," she snarled. "They know. And word will get out about you and your friends, as well."

Rob turned to Jorge and let some of the ugliness in his soul out.

"Edit out everything after the door exploded," Rob said. "That protects your cover and we can blame this mess on all on the troops I recruited. We'll send the tape to the Governor by courier, just before we blast off."

"You sure, kid?" Jorge asked.

"*In vino, veritas*, Jorge," Rob proclaimed.

And shot Lilijana once with the pulse pistol.

23

———

The voice over the intercom was sharp.

"Everyone either strap yourselves in or you get to have a medic fix you."

Rob figured that Raef could actually do this launch without all the theatrical craziness, but was putting on a show for the passengers.

Jorge and Roxy were in their cabins with the doors locked. It gave them plausible deniability later, depending on what Rob had to say now. Plus, Roxy needed a shower to get the blood and cordite out of her hair.

Rob was just going to have to burn his suit later. All the blood splatter was never coming out. Plus, he never wanted to be reminded of tonight. This was the first time he had ever had to actually shoot someone in his career, a painful failure of his training and charm.

He growled under his breath.

Twenty-six more men were aboard *Valencia del Oro* when it lifted than when it had landed. Rob was actually pretty impressed that all of them had managed to make the launch window when the signal arrived out of the blue in the middle of the night.

But then, he and Jorge had picked these veteran soldiers after Roxy had set the minimum range score acceptable.

The ship backed onto its lifters and slowly adjusted. Rob assumed Raef was lining the bow up before things got crazy, but you never knew with her. He had sat and hooked a seatbelt anyway. The others had, too, as soon as they saw him.

Fourteen of them were in the room with him here, including Nigel, with the rest stuffed into the two empty cabins for launch. The room was packed with adrenaline and macho, but Rob was the only one with dried blood on his face. Wasn't his, and he had specifically not wiped it off, just so these men immediately understood the situation.

Valencia del Oro stood on her ass and probably broke ever flight regulation *6940 Draconis* had on the books, but he really didn't care. Best outcome, he would never set foot in this system again, let alone on this planet.

Still, one more step in the plan complete.

Raef rode the engines hard. Somewhere in the vicinity of three and a half gees, standing on the engines. People didn't even talk because she had shut down the internal gravity and left them pressed against the aft wall of whatever cabin or seat they were in.

Didn't take long to get altitude at that burn. Raef rotated the ship back flat again after an hour by turning the grav-plates back on. They were still going up, but not at a mad dash now, so there could be some comfort.

"All hands, we will rendezvous with the carrier in forty-five minutes," Raef announced like it was a cruise ship or something. "You are now free to move about the designated chambers. Stay out of engineering, the bridge, or anyplace else you think I might shoot your sorry asses."

Yeah, Raef was a little miffed at having to haul so many people. But there was no quicker way to get off the planet and up to *Queen of the Borders*. They would have had to send a cargo tug and transport box down and equip it with enough life support to do the job. Something they had planned for later.

"Raef, am I on shipwide?" Rob asked casually, hearing his voice come bouncing out of the speakers.

She didn't bother answering.

"Everyone come to the kitchenette now," Rob said in a tired, angry voice.

The rest of his goon squad emerged and made their way aft fast enough. And Rob had forgotten that Longbow had brought guests as well. Jorge had told him, but Rob had lost it in the chaos of activating his troopers and getting to the ship.

Longbow first, followed by two women Rob didn't know, but night and day in height, beauty, and coloration. Three other men followed, so Longbow's cabin must have been crowded. The kitchen space was standing room only, and Rob had had a long day. Night. Experience.

"A little over four hours ago, a team rescued me from a group of folks that had wanted to ask some ugly, personal questions," Rob pitched his voice to carry to the band as well as the soldiers. "The bruise is mine, but none of the rest of the blood."

He paused to study everyone around him. Nigel always smelled like cordite, and now, so did Rob.

"We're going to change up the mission some from the original thing you were hired for," he continued. "If you feel the need to back out, I'll pay you for time, but not hazard pay, because I'll be leaving your ass up on the mothership when the rest of us do the mission."

A growl emerged from the room. No words, just a

challenge. None of these men were likely to back out or back down. They were just reminding him.

"The folks who captured me also sent a message to the place we're going to hit, which is why we're in a hurry," Rob growled back. "We can outrun the message, so they won't know we aren't there delivering pizzas."

That got a laugh.

"Once we're aboard the mothership, you will not talk to the crew, mostly because we've already got the two pods configured as troop transports and they don't have space for forty extra crew," Rob said. "Hopefully, none of you will be terrified of sleeping on air mattresses for a few nights."

More laughter.

Rob had studied the way Jorge did this. Even watched a few of the man's movies so he could crib the mannerisms and inflections.

Why learn from anybody but the best?

"What about us?" Longbow called over the heads of the soldiers.

"My understanding is that the third transport pod has been set up as a studio, within limits," Rob replied. Longbow knew this, but obviously hadn't shared everything with his team. "You'll have a week to yourselves, but you'll have to bunk in there for the most part. Again, lack of space."

And two of the only four women aboard either ship right now, plus Raef and Roxy, who he wasn't worried about.

"What's the operation, sir?" one of the older man close by asked.

"Originally, we were going to pull a con," Rob said with a smile that must have looked wretched, from the way folks reacted to the dried blood. "Sail up and pretend to have suffered a navigation failure that required mechanical assistance. Use that to drop you onto the surface of the moon, from which you would Trojan Horse those bastards."

"And now?" the man followed up.

"Jorge and Mrs. Jones will be leading a rapid assault, with you being organized into two teams," Rob said. "Like the script I talked about, but we're doing this in one take with live weapons."

"I'm sorry, sir," the soldier had a pained look on his face. "Did you say Mrs. Jones would be leading one of the teams? Does she even know how to shoot?"

Rob laughed so hard he cried before he could get his breath under control.

"All this blood on my face?" Rob asked the man. "There were three people alive in the room when her team blew the door, killing the man by the door and leaving another one in a side room for Jorge to shoot as her Entry Second. She killed all three of them herself with quick bursts while I was tied up and about to be executed."

Slightly stretching the truth, but only because Roxy wanted a prisoner that Rob killed.

"She's that good?" the man was aghast, but he looked like a local. One of the people that didn't think girls were dangerous creatures.

"By herself, she could probably kill three-quarters of you," Rob said.

"Oh, Rob, stop exaggerating," Roxy's sultry voice filled the room. "Remember, I set the minimum Hogan's Alley score for those boys to even be invited. That number was my average score. At my age, I could probably only take out two-thirds of them before somebody got lucky."

The casual way she said that, in that voice that was the wet dream of every boy who had ever heard it, and many of the girls, just seemed like frosting on the cake at this point.

Rob stood up and scowled mightily at them.

"I owe these bastards a ration of pain," he said simply. "You're going help me collect on a debt. Any questions?"

There were none at this point.
Go in and kill some people.
Just like pirates.

24

Longbow made his weary way forward, making the gravity transition from the neck of the mothership into the transport pod that was, for now, a commune and recording studio. Not a particularly great studio, as those things went, but they'd been able to hang some blankets and position some gear to get a pretty good concert hall reverb going, once they moved the microphones around.

The forward end was the personal space, with bunks and a portable head that had been stolen from somewhere and installed here long before Jorge Royo came along. Probably for people smuggling, if you put enough boxes down at that end.

It gave them privacy. But it also isolated him and the band, so every face was turned his way when he got the hatch opened and entered.

"Grab chairs," he announced in a tired voice.

They had been recording like mad. Really, like folks possessed by literal demons for the last several days. On top of that, regular planning sessions with the team and all the extras that had been hired.

Naomi slid a mug of fresh coffee into his hands as he planted his butt and drew a heavy breath.

"Okay, we're at the point where everything has to be on the table," Longbow said, studying faces around him. The rest were a little stir crazy, but that was the life of the touring musician. Too long in too cramped a space with constant practice and being in people's pockets all the time. Nothing new.

"From here, things will get a little messy," he continued. "We don't know how far behind us the alert message is, so we're going to come out of JumpSpace as hot as we can and go straight to the assault. Jorge thinks they aren't going to be at military alert, so their first warning might be shit blowing up."

"What's our role here?" Naomi asked.

She had turned into the speaker for the rest, even though it probably should have been Alicia. But Naomi had brought the rest of them in, so it was still her gig.

"You have nothing to do," Longbow replied, fixing her with a tired smile. "I'll be with one of the assault teams."

"Really?" Naomi asked, obviously both concerned and confused.

"So there's a lot the rest of you don't know," Longbow blew out a breath. "And didn't need to know. And maybe still don't. Jorge needs to know, though, so I have to ask."

He paused, looking for the right words. It was hard. He did other people's words, like an actor, rather than his own. Naomi's most recently.

"I can tell you more, but then you're on the inside, and you can't really ever get back out," Longbow continued. "You can leave, but people will watch you for the rest of your lives, and come after you if you talk. That's the kind of trouble brewing. I think we've got a good thing here, and would like to turn you into a touring band and maybe do more than one album, if we can make it work. But there will be people with guns, and you can probably never go back to *6940 Draconis* again after this. At least with your current identity."

They were silent. Probably shell-shocked, but that was fine. Nobody was immediately demanding to be let off this ride. At least they knew how crazy it might get before it was done.

"So you have to decide right now," Longbow continued. "If you're all in, I can tell you more. If any of you aren't then nobody finds out until much later."

One by one he went around the group. Alicia nodded, but she saw a bright future where this album made her rich and catapulted her into the big leagues of record producers, especially after Levi made some calls to some folks. Pepe just nodded. Dutch smiled, but the old man had already been everywhere and seen everything, and probably didn't figure he had that many years left to worry about looking over his shoulder either way.

Wolfgar scowled hard. Took Longbow's measure. Then the rest of the group. Finally turned to Naomi.

"You good?" he asked her.

Wolf had known her the longest. And been her first call when Longbow asked.

Naomi nodded to the man.

"I'm in, man," Wolfgar exhaled.

Naomi had as serious an expression as Wolf, but she was looking for something more than the rest of them were. For them, it was just an extended gig. A tour that would probably make them a lot of money and put them into a new circle of craft.

"I want more," she said quietly.

"I can't write," Levi replied "I can play, and entertain, but that's about it. I need a partner, but that's going to be a hard road. That's why there hasn't been one before. Didn't know anybody tough enough to survive it."

"And you think I can?" she asked carefully.

"I do, but you'll be stuck with me at that point," he said. "All the craziness you've seen and heard is nothing on the real story, but if you're in, you'll have to know everything, eventually."

"I've got time to learn it," she smiled at him.

Levi sighed.

"Thank you," he said. "Here's the part you'll never believe."

So he told them about the traffic accident that nearly killed him. The time in the hospital. Learning to walk again. Talk again. Play again. The second career as a medic, since he had already spent so much time learning how his own body was rebuilt.

Jorge Royo and the Service. That got a round of gasps, as the implications of him being a spy sank in. Levi didn't go into any detail, other than to explain how many missions he had done for Jorge, for Handsome, and for other folks.

"A traveling band is just about the best cover there is," Levi concluded. "Lots of gear in big boxes that only get looked at perfunctorily. Oversized personalities distracting folks from the real game. And we're rock stars, so everyone's fawning over us constantly."

"And Handsome Rob is a spy for *Lincolnshire*?" Naomi asked in a tiny voice.

"We all are, now," Levi let his gaze roam about the group.

They had signed up for crazy. Now they were beginning to understand the scope of things.

"So what about us?" Alicia asked, encompassing the rest of the group.

"I'm hoping I can convince you to stay on as band manager, in addition to engineering goddess and backing vocals," Levi smiled. "These three don't want any adult responsibilities."

He pointed at the boys, who all smiled back. Levi didn't really want adult responsibilities, either, but he could fake it appreciably well.

"You and Naomi can be in charge of things, and we'll handle the musical end of the equation."

That brought a smile to Naomi's face. And a second smile she and Alicia shared. Probably a promise of all the trouble they'd get into.

Levi didn't bother telling them that they would both get to go through something like an abbreviated Field Agent school if they were really in. He'd survived it. Handsome and Jorge and Roxy had thrived. Wolf, Pepe, and Dutch would just have to sign confidentiality agreements with really rough damage clauses.

It was almost like joining a *Salonnian* Syndicate and becoming a made man, when you got right down to it. But Levi could see the album taking shape under Alicia's hands. *Longbow* had caught a cultural zeitgeist to the point that it was in the top three selling albums of all time on more planets than he could count.

This new thing wasn't going to repeat that, but it was a better story. And would probably make them all rich.

Levi just wanted to play.

"So, we've got three days to nail it down," Levi announced. "Then the assault. I don't wanna be dead, but if I am, at least you'll have something to sell. Next week, we'll be going to *Lincolnshire* and inventing new lives, so plan accordingly."

They all would be. Even one used-up, nearly forgotten rocker.

25

———————

HANDSOME ROB WONDERED IF THEY'D BE ABLE TO HIRE *Queen of the Borders* for some sort of extended, semi-official thing when they got back, just so they could actually film parts of the movie with Captain Kedzierski playing something more of an anti-hero turns golden role. Rob already had a good idea in his head how to set up a rogue Tactical Officer as a double agent, although in real life, she had been following orders.

Never let the truth get in the way of a good story. Casting would be a bitch, so they might have to go actually get a real actress, and coach her into the role, since *Queen* didn't have any female crew. But just having Rodderick Kedzierski's growl down as things got tough and ugly would sell tickets, according to Jorge.

Rob hadn't bothered learning too many names on this ship. He, Jorge, and Roxy were in the Captain's office with the man, while the First Officer, Giles Rodriguez had the bridge. The only two others present were Hachiro and Ganesh, the two team sergeants that had emerged from training and meetings.

Everyone called them the Lucky Twins, since Hachiro meant Eighth Son, which was considered luck, and Ganesh was the ancient, Hindu god of wisdom and luck."

Soldiers and sailors were equally superstitious.

"You've done this sort of thing before," Kedzierski accused Jorge as Rob watched impassively.

Jorge took a sip from his ever-present, ever-full martini glass. Seriously, how did he manage that?

"If we had access to the old library, I'd show you the movie I made ten years ago, Captain," Jorge purred magnificently. "Almost exactly this ending, except we had to go in and rescue a space princess before the villain could arrive to marry her and ruin the woman's reputation and defile her purity. Strong Hindu overtones in that one."

Jorge said that last to Ganesh with a smile.

"And you think we'll be able to just land and waltz right in?" The captain wasn't convinced.

"If the message hasn't arrived, I think they'll be more relaxed about things," Jorge said. "We come out on the back side of the moon, launch the two tugs with boxes, with the third one flying escort. We swoop in low, come over the horizon at full speed, and land right in the middle of the landing field, where they can't shoot anything big at up without hitting their own fighters and gunships, parked up on the surface. Two teams blow the gun tower and the flight control tower. After that, we can either capture everyone as prisoners, or keep blowing shit up while Handsome and Nigel film everything."

"And me?" the man growled.

"If he doesn't have ground or air defenses, I expect you might be able to sail right overhead at an absurdly low altitude for a mothership, blasting away with your big guns. Same with the tugs. When was the last time *Queen of the Borders* got to be the Goddess of War, Kedzierski?"

"Never, and you know it, Royo." Those eyes got dangerous. "What happens if the messenger arrives?"

"If he's in an unarmed courier, you might as well capture it and steal his ship," Jorge grinned like a shark. "If it turns out to be *Wild Duck*, my crew and I would appreciate you staying around long enough to evac us off the surface, and then we'll run like hell. I can't imagine *Wild Duck* would be welcome back at *Draconis*, if he's really been a *Salonnian* spy all these years, but that's up to the Governor and whoever else you want to tell. Simple?"

"Oh, it sounds it," the man had a grim smile. "But these things never work out that way."

26

————

THEY HAD LITERALLY FLIPPED A COIN, AND ROB WAS
with Roxy's team, working with Ganesh and fourteen others.
Jorge had the smaller team, but he was taking out flight
control, so they were expecting criminal bureaucrats rather
than hooligans with guns. Longbow would be with Jorge
until they had casualties.

The planet was a moon circling a medium-sized gas giant
right out at the edge of the Iceball range from the star. There
was just enough atmosphere overhead to twinkle stars, but
not even enough to pick up dust and swirl it on a wind.

The base was right over on the edge of the terminator,
where the moon was tidally locked with the gas giant,
meaning the parent always appeared low on the horizon like
a malevolent eye peeking over the horizon. The local sun was
a really bright star that rose and set, but didn't warm things
much. The gas giant actually kept the surface not all that far
below water freezing, had there been any.

At least those were the images and details the Service had
provided. They were on final approach now, and would see it
in all its glory shortly for themselves shortly.

The rock, Rob knew, was dead. Cindered, gray rock for the most part with some smoothing, just from the flow back and forth between planets. Rob couldn't imagine why anyone would want to live here, but he supposed that if you wanted a well-placed, secret base, beggars couldn't be choosers.

Everyone was in combat suits for this. Semi-rigid armor over a regular space suit, so you could move around quickly without the risk of tearing something. Bullets or beams would still penetrate, but everyone was equipped with patch kits to keep away from death pressure.

The do-or-die portion sucked, but the men were all getting paid well, and the rest of them were *Lincolnshire* agents. Apparently, Levi had even initiated his band into the secret, but Rob and Jorge hadn't had a chance to really work out what that might mean to future missions, if the Service decided that the *Can't Shoot Straight Gang* was needed.

Rob hefted his camera and looked around at the men, and woman. They had all brought their own suits to this, so no two soldiers looked alike. At Jorge's insistence, everyone had a blue stripe across the forehead of their helmet, going all the way around like a crown. That told you who to not shoot at, hopefully.

The transport box was already in vacuum, so everyone was buttoned up tight.

"Weirdest damned thing I've ever been part of," Ganesh grumbled over the comm, looking over at Roxy in her skin-tight, sexy, golden suit.

She just smiled up at the man.

"I get weirder things in my breakfast cereal, sergeant," she replied.

She had her bolter rifle, but nobody but Rob had seen her use it in action. The rest of the team was about an even mix between pulse rifles and bolters, depending on their previous experiences with sand, dust, rain, and such. Pulse rifle was a much better weapon, when it wasn't raining. Bolts didn't care.

"All hands, this is the bridge," Kedzierski's voice suddenly came over comms. "Four minutes to horizons."

They had broken out of Jump nearly two hours ago and had been under a strict radio silence as their tugs carried them down to the deck and then started to race across the surface of the moon. Coming out of the gas giant, as it were, instead of out the sun on a regular planet.

Hopefully, that would mess up scanners. At least long enough.

Everybody stood now. Stretched kinks out of arms and legs. Checked weapons one last time.

Like most of the rest, Rob had a pistol on his thigh, in case he needed it. He would just be filming things, hopefully. If they could get any sort of movie out of this, everyone's covers would be fine, as most folks would chalk everything else up to Jorge being even weirder than most actors.

Roxy stepped close and motioned Rob to bend down. He touched faceplates with her and noted the wicked gleam in her eyes.

"Make sure you get several gratuitous shots of my ass, Handsome," she said, laughing.

"How about now?" he replied.

She nodded, and Rob stepped well away from her. He started filming by centering her bottom in the viewfinder and just lingering there. It truly was a fantastic ass on any woman, let alone one in for early forties. He zoomed slowly, letting her turn slightly and rock her weight enough to flex all those muscles. As he got closer, she turned some more, until you had a long shot of where her breasts would be, if not for all the plates and armor in the way, rendering them more imaginary than anything.

Finally, he got to her face. She was leaned forward

enough that he could keep the camera below her heroically as her face grew serious and intense. Mrs. Jones again, and not Roxy playing her.

"All right, men," she said into the camera. "They think they're safe from us here. Who would ever do something so insane, just for revenge? Sergeant, what's the count?"

"Fifteen locked and loaded, ma'am," Ganesh said in an equally serious voice.

"Very good," Mrs. Jones exclaimed. "If they aren't us, they aren't friendly, boys. Prisoners would be nice, but not necessary as there is nothing here they can tell us. We need to get in and kill that gun tower so the rest of the force can land and take this base. Everyone stand ready."

Rob held the shot for a few seconds as she looked beautiful and deadly.

"And cut," Rob said. He turned to Ganesh and stepped slightly to one side, kneeling to make the man look huge. "Rolling. Repeat your line in two seconds, Ganesh."

"Fifteen locked and loaded, ma'am," the sergeant repeated.

Around him, the men amped up their swagger a notch.

"Cut. Perfect," Rob called.

He rose and moved to the outer hatch. Mrs. Jones followed, and the others shifted. Ganesh stayed at the far end, where he would be the last man out, save for the camera.

"Okay," Rob called. "Everyone confirm that your face and helmet cameras are on right now. Don't worry about anything at that point, except looking tougher and meaner than everyone out there. We'll edit all that footage as we need to, and then come back later with lines for you to speak as overdubs, once we get home and are doing this on a soundstage. This will be one take. The hatch opens and I'll capture her leading you. Each man will follow in order, and

I'll get you as you go by. I'm the last one out, and I'll be blind, carrying this camera, so I would appreciate you boys killing anybody that might shoot at me. Deal?"

That got a lot of laughter and ribbing. He didn't bother telling them that Jorge had written those lines a week ago to motivate them, and he would be saying the exact same speech to his team. These men needed to concentrate on their jobs.

Rob was busy protecting the team's cover as actors.

The transport pod suddenly lurched a little and everyone stumbled.

"Ten seconds to ground," a man's voice came over the comms. "Stand by."

The space got as quiet as the tomb.

There wasn't enough atmosphere out there that the sound of weapons would travel, unless a beam him them, so Rob was just as well that it was quiet. He knelt and turned on the camera, again tracing Mrs. Jones from knees to gorgeous face, except she was ignoring him now, staring at the hatch she would open shortly, leading a charge of armed maniacs across a dark, quiet field to commit mayhem.

Not exactly why he had signed up for the Service, but sometimes you didn't have much choice about how to save the galaxy. Any little thing he could do help to bring down the criminal syndicates of *Salonnia*.

The box lurched as the tug put them on the ground.

"We're down," Mrs. Jones announced to her team and the audience. "Follow me!"

She threw open the hatch as Rob pulled the focus back several notches. Out she went, followed by the next man in quick order. One by one, until only Ganesh was left, and he went through at a hard jog.

Rob slung the camera up on his shoulder, adjusted the viewfinder, and chased Roxy into battle.

27

―――――――

Levi hadn't done this in a while, but it was like riding a bicycle, as long as you didn't faceplant before you remembered where the pedals were. He was about two-thirds of the way back in the line of soldiers as Nigel filmed everybody exiting, with a pistol in one hand and his overstuffed messenger back filled with first aid gear in the other. On his belt, he had three temporary shelters he could inflate, in the event of casualties. Hopefully nothing he would use today.

Roxy's team was at one corner of the landing field, and he and Nigel were at the other, just because the control tower and the defense tower were so far apart. As he followed in the wake of Jorge's raiders, Levi noted that the locals had started the process of digging some underground facilities, but hadn't gotten too far yet. Everything everywhere was above ground right now, including one medium-sized hangar building off to one side, where presumably starcraft crews could work on a ship in atmosphere. It looked big enough to hold two Starfighters at once, or maybe one bigger craft, like the tug and cargo pod he had ridden to get here.

The nearest garage door was suddenly punctured as the tug behind him opened fire with their turret gun. Levi knew it was them because there was just enough air to fluoresce under the power of the bolt passing overhead. Most of the buildings would be too reinforced to damage like that, unless you were just going to blow them apart and let everyone inside die in vacuum. As it was, the garage had to be taken out before anybody could launch a fighter at them.

Jorge's orders had been specific: Neutralize the place without killing anyone more than needed it. Right now, that meant taking the control tower and spiking the guns. *Queen of the Borders* would be coming over the horizon shortly and could engage any fighters that got off the ground. But until then, the ground teams would be slaughtered

At least that was the theory. Levi was just a guitarist and combat medic. He hadn't killed a tenth as many people as Jorge or Roxy in his career. Hell, Handsome was the only person who had killed fewer, exactly one, but that was because the kid was only just getting started.

Of course, if the new album was as good as he thought it might be, Levi wondered if he'd have to retire from the Service and go legit.

If only his mother could see him now, he laughed to himself.

No more outbound fire from the tugs. They needed to hide behind intact Starfighters on the field until the tower couldn't shoot anymore, on the belief that the locals wouldn't immediately blast their own landing field and destroy everything. They would get there, once they started to panic, but that was later.

Hit them hard now and eliminate their options.

Jorge was against a door in the side of the ugliest, gray anthill Levi could remember. Huge, but men were ants here. Alarms were sounding on various channels in the background, but Levi was ignoring most of it. The call he needed to hear would be for a medic. Hopefully, it would not come today.

Everybody outside were in suits, so Nigel blew the door apart with one of his rockets, after people quickly ducked away from any flying slivers of metal that might puncture even these suits.

That was one way to get everyone's attention. Nothing like a breach warning on top of fire alarms and intruder alerts. Rouse the dead, sort of thing.

Everyone poured through the now-obliterated airlock, Hachiro coming last, with a hand on Levi's back as the gunner was watching the rear flanks.

Inside, it was even uglier. Seriously, did they work at that, or was it just the outcome of bad culture? His music had never sold all that well in *Salonnia*, so he knew they had no taste at all, but this architecture was hideous.

Or maybe they just had a thing for hallways that sloped in at the top. That would give the rooms on the other side a strange vaulting effect, especially if everything felt like stretched hexagons, instead of perfectly functional rectangles.

Weirdoes.

And the lighting was too bright, even without atmosphere. A solid stream of light down the center of the room, so white it made his eyes hurt. Red lights flashed madly above up and down the hall.

Jorge had poured through a door, leaving three men here to guard the hallway. Levi moved past them and took up a spot in the stairwell out of the way, but close enough to support everything as Hachiro stayed at this end of the snake and got things organized.

Interestingly, three of these men were watching the open gap behind them, rather than the interior hallway. But that made a sort of sense. You'd need an airlock to get to them, and the building wasn't all that big. Someone might as well exit and circle the building as open a second hatch somewhere inside where they could sneak up on you.

They'd think of it, if Jorge gave them time. Too bad for them.

Something flashed and Levi found himself on his ass on the stairs.

He shook his head and stood up, realizing that there was enough atmosphere still to convey shock waves. And some asshole had just hit them with a rocket, or maybe lobbed a grenade into the hallway.

Hachiro was stunned but moving. The others were just recovering as well. Levi saw movement in the outside hallway.

He fired blind, not bothering to identify his target. Movement drew the barrel of his pulse pistol.

Worked. Somebody fell down. Wasn't wearing Jorge's blue crowns.

His team was still recovering. Must have gotten a flash/bang grenade in their laps and absorbed the pulse.

Levi swore and moved forward. He had no grenades. And someone on the other side had reacted too rapidly.

He dropped low and stuck his head around the corner after turning off the light on his helmet. Several more men were creeping forward, less than five meters away.

Levi shot the nearest one in the chest and ducked back. Bastards would probably put another grenade into the hatch as soon as they got organized.

Rather than wait, he threw himself forward, out onto the turf of the moon, and tumbled in the dust of the lunar surface. That kicked up a small puff of cloud that would hopefully distract them.

Turning, he fired at the nearest man, catching the guy just turning to see what had emerged.

A second shot as Levi walked fire down the line of ducklings. The third was finally turning enough to get a shot off, so Levi threw himself sideways. It worked. The shot missed.

But he fell on a big rock he hadn't seen in the semi-darkness, and dropped his pistol. Without light, he couldn't see it, either, leaving him down on his hands and knees in the dirt and about to get shot. Bastard over there saw the situation and paused to aim.

This was going to suck.

Hachiro stepped out of the hatchway and shot the man with a bolter rifle. It was an ugly way to die, since the holes went all the way through you and your suit. And four shots meant the guy was dead before his body stopped falling.

Levi found his pistol and scampered back to cover, pausing to grab some grenades from the first man he had shot.

"I thought you said you were the harmless one, Longbow," Hachiro ribbed him as they got to relative safety.

"I am," Levi smiled at the man. "You haven't seen Jorge or Mrs. Jones in action."

"Crap," the sergeant laughed. "Now I'm not sure I want to."

"Hey," Jorge's voice came over the comm. "Could you to pay attention? I'm expecting a counter-attack shortly."

"You missed it, boss," Levi laughed. "Four men with grenades and surprise, but we got them all. How's the top?"

"Neutralized," Jorge said. "Damn, we must be getting old. They shouldn't have reacted that fast."

"Hire a better script consultant next time," Levi replied.

"Hold on. Go ahead, Mrs. Jones," Jorge said.

"I said, the guns are out of commission," Roxy repeated in a tetchy voice. "Have these stupid mooks surrendered yet?"

"I'm working on finding out who's in charge now," Jorge said.

Long gap of silence.

"Longbow, did you get everything on helmet cam?" Jorge was back.

"Maybe," Levi said. "Wasn't really paying attention at that point."

"We'll review the footage later," Jorge growled. "But one of the guys you just shot was apparently the base commander. They're unhappy about giving up and think they can take us."

Levi started to say something, when the landing field suddenly exploded in light. Seriously, it was like dawn over Puerto Peñasco when you were too hung over to pull the curtains closed.

As the light faded, one of the Starfighters had exploded. A second one went up in flames a moment later, and then a third.

"Ground force, this is Command," Captain Kedzierski's calm, malevolent voice suddenly filled the airwaves. "Explain to them that I will continue annihilating their base until they do surrender. After the flight wing, I'll be going after the barracks with ship's cannon."

Levi stuck his head carefully out the hatchway and looked up. There was no real atmosphere, so *Queen of the Borders* had been able to fly incredibly low without much risk. Especially since nobody was looking up at the moment.

And, because the captain was like that, he had turned on all his running lights. A 1-Ring Mothership wasn't anywhere near the size of her big sisters, the 4-Rings, but she still looked enormous, flying above the base at barely five thousand meters elevation.

The night sky was just like those alien invasion vids,

when the invader suddenly emerges from the clouds and all hell breaks loose.

Levi held perfectly still and centered it in his cameras, figuring he had the best frame.

"That worked, Command," Jorge replied in a formal voice that would require some quick rewriting, but Levi knew was too good to pass up. "They're striking their colors now."

Levi let go a breath as general lights came on everywhere around the base, showing men in various stages of moving around in what had been the darkness just a moment ago. Some of them were pilots and crew who looked like they were getting ready to fly a suicide mission against the invasion, but nobody could do anything with a combat warship flying overhead.

Levi turned to head inside. He had three men with some level of trauma and they would need him.

28

Rob watched on a screen from the kitchen of *Valencia del Oro* as the last troop freighter lifted from the surface of *6725 Lacertae*. That was the third one, and the base itself was as abandoned as they could get the place.

If someone wanted to die with honor in the flaming wreckage, Rob was all out of patience to deal with them today.

Jorge and Roxy were matching each other for martinis, toasting one another lavishly for a mission well done. Nigel had gone back to his machine shop to try some experiment after watching his toys in actual combat. Rob had stuck with coffee for now.

As the freighter got high enough, *Queen of the Borders* let loose with her Type-3 beams on the base itself. It was almost like using a blowtorch on an anthill, as Longbow had said, but Rob had to agree with the imagery. And it worked. The buildings imploded as the beams converted energy to heat and overstressed the walls.

The landing field was one puddle of dead starcraft after

another, from one-man Starfighters up to gunships with a crew of ten. None of them had gotten off the ground in time. Captain Kedzierski had spiked them hard and fast. One gunship might not have been a threat to *Queen of the Borders*, but a handful would have been enough.

"Kid, you done good," Jorge turned his attention this way. "That was about as suicidal a mission as I've ever seen the Service hand anyone. You shouldn't have even survived, let alone pulled it off."

"I had help," Rob pointed out, gesturing to the two of them with his coffee mug.

"All we did was shoot people and talk," Jorge said. "You did the heavy lifting."

Rob shrugged. Maybe.

Before he could say anything, Longbow stepped into the forward hallway and started this direction. Naomi was with him, trailing a step as they came into the kitchen.

"You people are insane," Naomi said, after she filled her own coffee mug and sat on the end of the round booth, opposite Jorge. "You really did it."

"What's that liar told you?" Jorge demanded with mock severity.

"Enough," Naomi said. "Maybe too much. Probably nowhere near enough to completely understand."

"You do realize that your world has changed and that you can never go back?" Roxy asked.

"Yeah," Naomi turned to look at her. "But this was brass ring time, Mrs. Jones. Grab it and hold on, or forever regret it."

"So you think the band will work out?" Rob asked, aiming his question at both Naomi and Longbow.

He shrugged. She fixed him with a hard stare.

"Are you going to blow our cover as a rock band with some future mission, Handsome Rob?" she asked.

"No, but I'm going to probably use you to sneak in places where people like me aren't supposed to be," Rob answered. "The Service will see a tour as a fantastic opportunity to do unto to others, with the chaos confusing events."

"We have an album," Naomi shrugged in turn. "A band. A tour would be frosting on a perfect cake at this point. What will you need from us?"

By us, she made it clear that she was speaking for the other civilians forward, crammed into the two spare cabins, while Naomi was bunking with Levi. They would surface eventually, but Raef had ordered them to remain indoors until she made it JumpSpace.

"Keep him happy," Roxy spoke up. "Keep his ass in motion when he wants to slack off. Don't ask too many questions about things happening around you. And make more music."

"That I can do, Mrs. Jones."

"And in private, you can call me by my real name," Roxy said. "I'm not the real Mrs. Jones, but space is big and confusing. I'm Roxy."

"Roxy," Naomi repeated with a nod. "And the rest of you?"

"He really is Jorge Royo," Levi said with a grin. "That's an even better story than Roxy. Handsome is just an ordinary spy we picked up along the way."

"Excuse me?" Rob asked. "I'm far from ordinary, Longbow. Wait until I get involved with your publicity team back home."

"So we're going forward?" Naomi asked. "I mean, most of my life is boxed up and stored in the cargo bay aft, same as everyone else. But we're headed to *Lincolnshire*?"

"We are, young lady," Jorge pronounced. "When we get there, that's when the adventures start."

Rob nodded.

He had been sent out to do the impossible, and somehow had managed to succeed. And he could come back to *Ramsey* with a rock band, an album to distribute, and a tour to plan.

The galaxy wouldn't know what hit it.

29

—————

Levi felt Naomi's warm hands wrap around his chest from behind as she pressed herself up against him.

"It's okay," she murmured. "Just a nightmare. You're awake now. You're safe. I'll take care of you."

He found the cabin as it had been when he went to sleep. No monsters at the foot of the bed, dragging him off to Vishnu knows where. No nightmares, like Naomi had said.

He rolled inside her arms and touched foreheads with her.

"Sorry," Levi said. "Didn't mean to wake you up."

"What happened?" she asked. "You haven't slept this badly before."

"Killing people brings the nightmares back," Levi murmured, an admission he hadn't made to anyone but his psychologist before this. The Service had one on staff, with his full history in file folders. It was a thick file by now.

"Was it bad?" she asked. "Down on the surface?"

"Roxy's team caught them with their pants around their ankles," Levi chuckled. "They were in the command room all by themselves because the guy on duty had taken a nap. *Queen* could had dropped us straight down, possibly."

"I meant you, Levi," she reached up a hand and caressed his face.

"I had to shoot three men," Levi finally said out loud. "They had snuck up on my team and taken out the guys right behind me. So I attacked them."

"You took out three armed men by yourself?" she pulled back a little in shock to look at him. "I thought you were a medic?"

"I am," he laughed. "Only people that needed me were the ones I killed and a few others. Didn't save anybody while we were on the surface."

"So what do you need?" she asked, pulling him close against her chest.

He could feel her heartbeat echoing his through the shirts they both wore.

"You," Levi finally realized. "Keeping me warm. I can face anything as long as I have that."

She kissed him. It felt good.

He'd been by himself for decades, even when he wasn't sleeping alone. Killed more people in the name of the Service than almost anybody he knew. Almost.

Nowhere near Jorge or Roxy, but that was about it. Most agents went their entire careers and never even drew a weapon.

He just wanted to play guitar and sing.

Maybe, finally, he could.

ABOUT THE AUTHOR

Blaze Ward writes science fiction in the Alexandria Station universe: The Jessica Keller Chronicles, The Science Officer series, The Doyle Iwakuma Stories, and others. He also writes about The Collective as well as The Fairchild Stories and Modern Gods superhero myths. You can find out more at his website www.blazeward.com, as well as Facebook, Goodreads, and other places.

Blaze's works are available as ebooks, paper, and audio, and can be found at a variety of online vendors (Kobo, Amazon, iBooks, and others). His newsletter comes out quarterly, and you can also follow his blog on his website. He really enjoys interacting with fans, and looks forward to any and all questions-even ones about his books!

Never miss a release!

If you'd like to be notified of new releases, sign up for my newsletter.

I only send out newsletters once a quarter, will never spam you, or use your email for nefarious purposes. You can also unsubscribe at any time.
http://www.blazeward.com/newsletter/

ABOUT KNOTTED ROAD PRESS

Knotted Road Press fiction specializes in dynamic writing set in mysterious, exotic locations.

Knotted Road Press non–fiction publishes autobiographies, business books, cookbooks, and how–to books with unique voices.

Knotted Road Press creates DRM–free ebooks as well as high–quality print books for readers around the world.

With authors in a variety of genres including literary, poetry, mystery, fantasy, and science fiction, Knotted Road Press has something for everyone.

Knotted Road Press
www.KnottedRoadPress.com

www.ingramcontent.com/pod-product-compliance
Lightning Source LLC
Chambersburg PA
CBHW070302120726
47910CB00007B/2348